THE WEIRWOODS

by
THOMAS BURNETT SWANN

A Division of Charter Communications Inc.
A GROSSET & DUNLAP COMPANY
1120 Avenue of the Americas
New York, New York 10036

THE WEIRWOODS

Copyright ©, 1967, by Ace Books, Inc.

A slightly different version of this novel was serialized in *Science Fantasy* #77, 78, and is copyright ©, 1965, by *Science Fantasy*.

All rights reserved. No part of this book may be reproduced in any form or by any means, except for the inclusion of brief quotations in a review, without permission in writing from the publisher.

An ACE Book

Cover art by Stephen Hickman

Printed in U.S.A.

The serval cats surrounded her couch. Of course! They had come to shield her on this night of strangeness and fear. She was not surprised when gentle Bast, the leader of the cats, sprang onto the couch and placed an affectionate paw on her arm. Often he slept beside her and laid his head against her cheek.

He prodded her with his paw. Then he mounted her body and peered into her eyes. He was a heavy animal; it was hard to breathe with the weight of his pressing claws. She felt the heat of his breath and smelled an acrid, salty scent which she did not recognize. He looked somehow—alien. Slowly, with deliberate grace, like a trained leopard in a circus, he raised his paw.

Slowly, with ever-growing horror, she realized that the prodding paw, the slow advance, and the fixedly staring, hypnotic eyes, were gestures shrewdly calculated to tease and torture her. His eyes were as cold as a topaz. Perhaps they had always been cold. But now she was able to read them without the sentimentalizing haze of her affection, and she grasped the terrible truth that love can never be compelled, from man, from sprite, from beast; that one who loves, however she longs for requital, however long she waits, may receive in return the reverse of what she gives.

And now she recognized the smell on the animal's fur. It was blood.

I

ETRUSCAN SUTRIUM: the city beside the forest. She crowned a cliff which became an island in spring, when torrents of melting snow descended from blue Mt. Cimini and clawed at her base with icy talons; and in summer she remained an island, but ringed with verdure—bracken and tangling ivy—which licked the wounds of spring with healing tongues. To the north, the forest crouched like a cat. The Ciminian Forest, it was called on the maps of the region, but the townspeople whispered another, more sinister name: the Weirwoods. Weird Woods? Werewolf Woods? No one remembered the origin of the name, but everyone felt the threat in those cryptic, joined words, and the Sutrii girdled their city with walls of square tufa blocks; with battlemented towers; and with three arched gateways, the largest of which opened to the south, the fortunate region, the abode of the rural gods. Basalt roads descended in sweeping curves from each of the three gateways and joined, below the southern gate, at a drawbridge which spanned the moat. At the north of the town there stood not a gate but a watchtower whose square, stone-lidded eye eternally fixed the forest in its unblinking gaze.

Actually, Sutrium was a town and not a city, neither Veii of the fiery forges nor Caere of the bronze chariots nor many-streeted Tarquinia, but a town whose affluence nonetheless glittered in its temples—the circular shrine to Tages, the Divine Infant—the great orange rectangle to Jupiter, Juno, and Minerva (or, as the Etruscans called them, Tinia, Uni, and Menerva); and in the vigor of its people, the men in loincloths, their sun-bronzed shoulders more beautiful than any cloth, the women swathed to their feet by linens and wools embroidered with Gorgon's head and winged Chimera, she-wolf and bird of prey. *Surely we are blessed by the gods,* they seemed to boast, *striding like sunbeams to show our scorn of the forest; attended by slaves whose sleek, splendid nakedness testifies that they are generously fed and yet without possessions, that they live well by our bounty but live to serve our whims.*

Even the cats of Sutrium were glossy with bee-colored fur: golden, with ebony spots and rings. They were not the domestic cats of Egypt, but the large serval cats of Africa, trapped in the jungle by the Carthaginians, who sent them as gifts to their Etruscan allies. They followed their masters into the marketplace and sniffed disdainfully at the barbarous country folk who came to trade, with starved, thin-legged dogs pattering at their heels. They drowsed on stone couches in courtyards where soft-padding slaves with tiny, leaf-shaped trays of beaten silver served them the cheese of snow-white heifers or the wings of carefully plucked pheasants.

In truth, the dwellers in the forest, the Weir Ones, appeared to offer no threat to this town of affluent citizens, obedient slaves, and pampered cats. Every ninth day, the Sutrii allowed the Weir Ones to enter the town and make purchases in the marketplace: red-figured vases imported from the kilns of Athens; figured brocades from the looms of Miletus; bronze daggers smelted in the forges of Veii. The Sutrii tolerated these unwashed rustics because of the chestnuts which they brought from the forest in wicker baskets; the fresh venison and the pots of honey; the tender eels from Lake Ciminus.

In return for the right to trade in the marketplace, the Weir Ones allowed the Sutrii access through the Weirwoods to Viterbo and Volsinii and other Etruscan cities of the north. Long ago, it was said, they had also offered access to the heart of the forest and their own Sylvan cities. But the ancestors of the present Sutrii had scorned the offer and passed through the forest with the look of aristocrats in a foul- smelling compound of slaves. Thus, the Weir Ones no longer sought them as friends. Still, they allowed them to follow the one path—and claimed in return the right to trade.

In the marketplace, the Weir Ones seemed shy, halting, and clumsy; in the forest, when glimpsed from the Road, they seemed to have put on strength, like a god who had donned a mantle of invulnerability. The backs of the Centaurs arched in manly pride and their clattering hooves became the beat of drums; the horns of the Fauns curved like daggers of bone. Such glimpses were not reassuring to those who traveled the Road. If riding in carriages, they shut their eyes and imagined the forest to be inhabited solely by naked and compliant nymphs. As a matter of fact, there were many nymphs in the forest, the female Water Sprites, usually naked, always compliant to males of their own race, but liking the Etruscans no better than a dolphin likes a shark.

Lars Velcha of Spina was bringing his daughter and his slaves to live in Sutrium, where his late brother, Appius, had bequeathed a villa to him. His wife and his son were dead, slain two years ago by a raiding party of Gauls. He had tried to forget them; or, since forgetting was plainly impossible, to avenge them by driving the red-haired raiders back to their mountains and offering the heads of captives to the dark-winged Vanth, goddess of death. But vengeance was not an opiate for grief. In the town of his birth, boyhood marriage, and fatherhood, he met the loss of love with every turn of a street where his wife had walked like a phoenix in her robes of fire; with every field where his young son had wrestled or drawn a bow or hurled a discus. Sutrium offered, if not forgetfulness, at least the dulling of unfamiliarity.

"You must pass through the Weirwoods tomorrow," the innkeeper had said, visibly awed by the presence of so great a nobleman and, at the same time, wishing to impress him with a knowledge of the countryside. "Take care not to leave the Road. The Weir Ones are vigilant, you know."

Lars Velcha had laughed. "You think I'm afraid of a few scurvy Fauns? My brother has told me about them straggling into the market. Barefoot. Broken horns. Chunks of copper to spend instead of coins, like the peasants we rule in Rome."

But Lars, if sometimes a foolhardy man on the battlefield and a boastful man with a cup of wine in his hand, was not a father to risk his daughter's life. Once he had entered the forest, he was careful to keep his party on the Road. Two naked slaves, armed with clubs, rode at the head of the column; he, with Tanaquil dreaming at his side, drove a carriage—*carpentum*, it was called—with bronze wheels and rounded leather hood; and three wagons driven by slaves and laden with tripods, braziers, candelabra, scrolls, clothing, and weapons brought up the rear. There was no temptation to stray from the path. The bordering trees made barbed palisades, which bore their greenery as if with reluctance, as if they expected to wrestle it from their limbs and fling it down like a netting over the path. Elms and chestnuts, beeches and oaks, and trees of ill omen too: buckhorn, black elder, and butcher's broom. In places, the Road grew disheveled with grapevines, which ground under the wheels like human limbs, and with spiky branches, split and charred by Tinia's lightning.

Placid Tanaquil rode in silence. Nothing it seemed, could shake her, not trees of ill omen nor lightning-blackened limbs. Sleepy-eyed, soft voiced, rounded of arm and breast to the point of voluptuousness, she combined a woman's body with a child's indolence. She was seventeen; since the death of her mother and brother, she had almost ceased to grow except in her body. She lived, it seemed, in a long and rarely broken dream from which she emerged with reluctance to eat or speak or sit at the loom, and to which she returned like the sheep in Sappho's poem, "back to the welcome fold." Now, in her stillness, she might have been an image of Persephone, the Maiden, crowning a wooden temple. If she saw the forest at all, it was only to watch a sunbeam alchemizing the leaves or a blue-eyed owl drooping among the branches.

"Tanaquil," he said at last. "Hand me the flask. The sun has given me a thirst."

Nodding, she handed him a silver flask encased in wicker and filled, presumably, with muscatel, the favorite Etruscan drink.

"Tanaquil," he sighed, upending the flask.

"You've drunk it already," she smiled.

"There was none to drink. You forgot to fill it at the inn."

Her lazuli-colored eyes widened with remorse. "Father, forgive me!"

"Never mind. We're sure to cross a stream before long. I will drink then."

"The slaves have flasks. Borrow one of theirs."

He looked at her with stern reproval. "Slaves' flasks are for slaves' lips." Sometimes her democratic fancies, dropped on the air as innocently as dew from leaves, disturbed and astonished him—fancies, no doubt, imbibed from Athens. A gifted race, the Athenians—their sculpture was second to none—but newfangled in their politics. Democracy indeed! They would soon yearn for a tyrant.

But the mention of flasks increased his thirst.

In a little while he said, "I think I hear running water. To the left."

"But you mustn't leave the Road," she cried.

Her vehemence startled him. "Why not?"

"You know what the innkeeper said."

"Charun take the innkeeper!"

"Send one of the riders."

"They can never find anything. Remember, they are Roman peasants. Ask them to find the brand on the back of their hands, and they'll point to a mole on their feet. I'll go myself." He patted her reassuringly on the wrist where a bracelet coiled in the shape of a leopard. As always, her beauty stirred him to pride that he, with his rugged, sword-scarred face, his black beard—black as the prow of a pirate's penteconter—and his aquiline, thrice-broken nose, had sired so flower-like a child. A net of fine-spun silver enclosed her hair, which rivaled the purple-blackness of wild grapes, and three scarlet poppies flared in the clustering curls. Poppies belonged to Vanth, the lady of death. But their redness was vital with life like Tanaquil's cheeks, which needed no touch of carmine to heighten their flush. *Like her flowers,* thought Lars, *my daughter is dead and alive at the same time, a passionate being wrapped in sleep. But when she wakes—*

He roared to the slaves on horseback: "Ho there, Marcus and Caelius. I am going to look for water. Keep an eye on my daughter." Marcus and Caelius grunted acquiescence. "Roman peasants," he muttered. "Stolid as pigs, stupid as sheep."

"Father," Tanaquil called after him as he hit the path, his sheathed dagger rattling at his side. He stopped and somewhat impatiently turned to face her.

"There is something in there."

"Of course," he laughed. "Birds, animals, Weir Ones."

"Something—not kind."

"Nothing in the forest is kind. But neither am I. Thus, I have nothing to fear."

But Lars, like most of his race, was superstitious and intuitive, and Etruscan men respected their women's intuitions. He paused in spite of himself. "Something—not kind." But he was thirsty, and proud.

He plunged up a ridge through thickets of trees and blackberry brambles which tore at his bare calves and arms—Etruscan tunics covered only the torso—and lodged in the linen fabric of his upturned shoes (womanish shoes, made for show, not wear! He ought to have worn his boots.) Arboreal darkness engulfed him as volcanic ashes engulf a town; the thrusting branches lashed his face. When he stumbled into a path, he felt as if lava had spewed him, scorched and gasping, into an aisle of refuge. Prints were visible in the crushed grass. Hoofprints. Of goat—or Faun? Of horse—or Centaur? The sound of water had become an importunate gurgling. Thirst, furry and sharp, pawed at his throat. He followed the prints.

And came to a lake. The sound he had heard was the lapping of water against the bank. He stood, transfixed by the spirit of the place, the genius loci. And troubled. Stretched like the tarnished silver of an old shield, it was not a lake for men. It was one of those places where divinity seemed to brood, articulate in the wind and ruffling the waters with giant fingers; scornful of all things human—weak, puny, and mortal.

But he was thirsty, and proud.

He could see, across the lake, the undulating rise of Mt. Cimini, her sienna-colored gorges rising into a smoke-blue peak. He could see the marshy shoreline to his left. But his view to the right was blocked by a wooded promontory jutting into the water like a huge fallen tree. The lake, he had heard—its name was Lake Ciminus—was inhabited by Water Sprites, and beyond that promontory, no doubt, lay boats and habitations.

Almost stealthily he knelt on the bank. Black eels bent with the current; fat pike drowsed among spear-straight reeds. He cupped his hands and drank of the water: acrid with sulphur but clean and quenching. He lowered his flask.

At the same time he saw the boy. At first he mistook him for a human boy, asleep on his back in the sun. Then, with the fascination of discovery, he discerned the copper skin, the pointed ears, the soft fins at the temples, the webbed feet, the thickness of silken fur on stomach and loins. A Water Sprite. A god, a credulous man would have said, but gods did not allow themselves to be surprised. He slept on the deck of a crude boat which was little more than a log flattened on top, with a raised canopy of boughs and wattle and a prow in the shape of an owl. It was partially hidden now; blended against the promontory like a natural extension. And yet the concealment was probably an accident. The sleeper would have no reason to fear invaders. He slept with confidence of his own lake, in his own land.

How old was he? Perhaps sixteen. The close-cropped hair on his head looked fine and soft. Flaxen, you might have said, except that its brilliance demanded a sumptuous adjective: silver. Not the lifeless silver of an old man's hair, but the bright electric burning of a dragonfly's wing or a thinly hammered goblet held to the sun. Slender and silver-gold, he lay like a tiger lily bent on its back. His lips curled to a smile; he seemed to be dreaming of sweet and sensuous things, his radiant boyhood poised, in memory or anticipation, on the threshold of maturity.

Tanaquil must see him too, thought Lars. *He will charm her out of her dream. I will take him back with me!*

He had always been served by slaves, and it seemed to him right and inevitable that some should rule and some should serve. When Etruscans—or Greeks—or Egyptians—required new slaves, they simply launched a war against their neighbors. In the case of a Water Sprite it was really a kindness to snatch him from the forest, with its quick lightnings and its foul-breathed wolves, to the safety of Sutrium; to feed and tend him in the bosom of a pleasant house.

Lars was a muscular man: the calves of his legs were as broad as coconuts. A seasoned warrior, however, he could move with the stealth of lynx. He glided into the water and toward the boat. The bottom was soft beneath his slippered feet, and the cool currents eased his travel-sore limbs.

He leaned to the boy as a father leans to his son, reluctant to break his sleep. The boy opened his eyes; their tawny, speckled gold held nothing of fear. Surprise, yes; that someone should dare to wake him. Surprise, and rage. Before the accusing eyes could shake his purpose, Lars enclosed him with rigid arms.

Never had he felt such strength in such slender limbs! He might have been wrestling a shark. He staggered, reeled, and, just as the sprite was wriggling out of his grasp, he struck the base of his neck with a quick, sharp blow. The sprite collapsed in the water, floating on his stomach and looking, pathetically, like an empty wine bladder. Lars lifted him onto his shoulder—how light he felt for one who had struggled so hard!—and headed for his carriage. With such a burden and without the use of his arms, it was hard to negotiate the blackberry thickets. He tore his legs on the thorns and once he raked a thorn across the sprite's bare shoulder but it left no mark; the skin must be very tough—water resistant, no doubt. He looked at the sprite's closed eyes, their revulsion masked by the lids. It was only a boy after all. Of course he had been enraged; of course he had fought like a shark! What boy wouldn't? But once in Sutrium, Tanaquil would gentle him into a docile companion. Before her unfailing calm, the harshest weapons must blunt and yield.

Tanaquil slipped from the carriage and, lively for once, ran to meet him. Eagerness flushed her face.

"Father," she cried, "You have found a Weir One! Has he hurt himself?"

"He is only stunned."

"*You* stunned him, didn't you?"

"I brought him back to be your playmate."

By now they had reached the carriage. Together they settled the boy in a nest of linen hangings which were destined to grace the doors of their villa in Sutrium. Tanaquil knelt beside him and placed a pillow, curled like a sleeping cat, under his head.

"A playmate," she repeated, her eyes traveling

nervously over his naked limbs. "But—he is more than a boy. I think you should take him back to the forest."

"Nonsense. If not a playmate, then your personal slave. We're doing him a kindness. What sort of life do you think he leads in the woods? Threatened by wolves and hunters?"

"There are no hunters in these woods. Till now."

The sprite began to stir. Coughing a little to rid his lungs of water, he blinked at Tanaquil. In the shadows of the carriage, the gold had left his eyes. Iron had taken its place: the iron of a Roman spear.

He spoke in a curiously accented but recognizable Latin, an ancient tongue familiar to Lars and Tanaquil because it belonged to Rome and other tributary cities of the Etruscan League. He said:

"You have stwayed."

"Strayed, he means," said Tanaquil, "He seems to have trouble with his 'r's."

"But why strayed?" demanded Lars. "We're right on the road to Sutrium."

"I think he means," said Tanaquil, "that you strayed from the Road when you went to the lake. You broke the agreement with the Weir Ones."

"Agreement? But that was centuries ago!"

The boy smiled: "My name is Vel." But his smile was not kind.

Tanaquil said, as if from a great distance: "Vel, you have the eyes of a cat."

II

BEFORE HIS DEATH, Tanaquil's uncle had shared her love for poppies. His garden in Sutrium burned with them; they branded the rocks, the narrow mouth of the grotto sacred to Lavis, god of underground springs, and the ridge of tufa stone which formed the back of the house. Red flowers and brown rocks; brightness and somberness: they seemed the measure of Sutrium and its people—of all Etruscans, moody, mercurial, who laughed at funerals and wept at banquets.

Tanaquil sat on a three-legged bench of stone and watched a dragonfly as it shot from a purple cyclamen with white-veined leaves to poise above a tangle of star-shaped clematis. Her mind seemed awash with a saffron haze which was scarcely distinguishable from the sun-washed afternoon, the tinkle of cowbells echoing from the fields below the town, and the cries of children rolling hoops in the street. Shut in the garden by a wall of bricks, she had shut herself in the smaller garden of her dream. She watched the dragonfly; became him, whirring above the incandescence of the flowers, the lifted scarlet chalices of the poppy, the prodigal constellations of the clematis.

She was not alone. She shared the garden with a serval cat, a languid, middle-aged male given to her by a friend of her late uncle. Bast, though twice the size of his Egyptian cousin, the temple cat, was no more inclined to movement than his mistress; like Tanaquil he appeared to enjoy a dream, though its nature was hard to guess from his yellow, expressionless eyes. Perhaps he was dreaming of pheasant wings and cheese. Tanaquil stroked him slowly, drowsily, and felt the fur, smooth like the pelt of a unicorn, ripple beneath her fingers.

A door croaked on its wooden hinges. Tanaquil raised her head and blinked with surprise. For an instant it seemed as if her dead brother, Aulus, were striding to meet her as he had two years ago when the party of Gauls had infiltrated Spina by way of the underground sewer.

Slim and boyish he had looked—he was just sixteen—but affecting a warrior's stride and bound on a warrior's mission. He had come to tell her that she must take refuge with the slaves in the atrium, while he went in search of their mother, who had gone to market with a single attendant. The Gauls, it seemed, were raging at large in the streets and scattering death with their big-bladed swords.

Just as he turned to leave her, she held him and kissed his cheek.

"You're only a boy," she said. "Don't go."

He looked at her with hurt eyes. "I'm a year

older than you, and a soldier."

He had found their mother and died defending her.

"Aulus," she gasped.

"Vel," he said.

His features, blurred with sunlight, hardened into clarity.

The Water Sprite. The slave. She had feared him from the day of his capture a month ago in the forest. He had never threatened her; he had rarely spoken her name. And yet she had made her father assign him to the kitchen—to serve red wine and pasta, black grapes and thrushes garnished with olives, to scour the floor with fuller's earth or barter for chickens in the marketplace; but never to enter her room or her father's room, in the way of personal attendants. In a house of a dozen slaves and as many rooms, it was not difficult to avoid him.

She turned her eyes from his offending nakedness. Etruscan women were used to the nudity of male slaves. But Vel disturbed her. Perhaps it was the soft fur which downed his stomach: the fur of a cat. Perhaps, the brown triangular fins which sprouted from his temples like misplaced horns, or the webbed feet which did not walk but padded wetly across the ground with a faint, unnerving squish. Once she had caught him wading in the compluvium, the small, square pool in the atrium which caught and stored the rain from the roof and served the family for drinking purposes; but at other times, when he could not possibly have wet his feet, he walked with the same oozing steps and one half-expected him to leave a slimy trail.

He extended a goblet of purple Phoenician glass. Its base was the fish-god Dagon; its curving stem, his tail.

"Your father has gone to the market. He asked me to bring you some hot wine and honey." His childish lisp invariably startled her; though at times he looked like a child, his voice was deep and guttural, and old like his eyes.

She took the goblet without looking at him.

He spun to leave the garden. There was something child-like about his narrow shoulders and slender flanks, and yet at the same time sexual. He made her think of the blatantly phallic Fauns which, young, grinning, sculptured in bronze, supported the tables in the triclinium or dining room.

It was wrong, however, to hurt him because of her fear.

"Vel," she said.

He turned to face her.

"Vel, I am sorry."

"For what?"

"For my father bringing you here. He meant to please me. But I never wanted you taken from your lake."

She searched her mind for something to say to him; to ease his loneliness. It did not occur to her to pity a slave, but Vel seemed less a slave than a prisoner. He always had the look of wearing a cage around his shoulders. He seemed to be straining against invisible wires.

"I was watching the dragonfly," she said, pointing to the cyclamen. "Earth and heaven—he has the best of both."

"Earth is best," said Vel—he pronounced it "uhth."

Quick as a cat, he caught the insect between his fingers and held him to Tanaquil as if he wished to make her a present. She had hunted dragonflies as a child. She bent her fingers to grasp the black, stiff body and spare the fragile wings, but Vel, as if he were shelling beans, snapped the body, peeled off the wings, and presented the pathetic remnants to Tanaquil in his open palm.

"Uhth is best," he said.

Hot ashes of anger exploded in her brain. She struck his hand and sent the fragments fluttering to the ground.

"Why did you do it?" she cried.

Her outburst seemed to surprise him. Perhaps he had grown accustomed to her lethargy.

"I do not know." he shrugged. "I meant to give him to you unbwoken. But you angered me.

"But how?" She almost wanted him to accuse her of slights and insults and thus to justify his cruelty.

"You never look at me. I wanted to shake your dweam."

"But I need my dream," she gasped. "Without it I feel—naked."

She did not see him move; or rather, she felt before she saw him: the coppery hardness of his mouth and body, the webbed toes snaking around her ankles, capturing her like tendrils of seaweed. Except for his toes, there seemed no softness anywhere in that slender, boyish body. Only a bruising, implacable hardness.

And yet she desired him. Words, images, glimpses out of her past, ignored at the time, returned to her now with bruising immediacy. The songs of the Fescennine singers, those bawdy players who traveled from town to town and sang the infidelities of the gods. The harvest festival of Liber, the earth-god, when a giant phallus was wreathed with ivy and carried in a procession through the streets. The look on the face of a slave girl watching a naked boy as he worked in the fields. She had listened and seen but, lost in her dream, she had failed to understand. Through the frank sexuality which permeated all phases of Etruscan life—the home, the theater, the circus, and the countryside—she had moved with the open but sightless eyes of a sleepwalking child.

The musky scent of him, acrid and sweet at once, assailed her nostrils and seemed to course through her blood like the hot borax hurled from the earth in the gorges near the coast. Her gentleness cried that he was hard and cruel, but her body solicited his cruelty.

Incredibly, it was her brother who saved her. When Vel had entered the garden, he had seemed to be Aulus, returned from the nether lands. Now, he seemed to her a caricature, a desecrating mockery of the boy she had loved. With a strength belied by the soft roundness of her limbs, she flung him away from her; or rather, flung herself out of his arms and toward the rock which enclosed the grotto; stumbling backwards, trampling poppies under her sandals; falling at last to her knees, ready to fend him off with upraised fists. He stood above her, hands on his hips, laughing. A phallic demon, proud of his manhood.

"You thought I was only a child," he said.

"No," she said. "I thought you were a cat."

"A cat," he mused, as if he considered the comparison to be a compliment. "Like him?" He pointed to Bast, drowsing among the cyclamen.

"No. A cat in the jungle."

"You have lost your flowers," he said, kneeling beside her to snap a black-hearted poppy from its stem and place it teasingly in her hair.

A gay, sudden music rang in the streets: the pipe of a double-flute, the rhythmical rolling of wheels, the thudding feet of a heavy animal. Vel straightened and peered at the garden wall. His pointed ears quivered like maple leaves in a gust of wind. His face, so recently cruel, softened to radiance. He looked as if he were going to purr. Instead, he raced to the edge of the garden and, catching the wall with his hand, vaulted onto the top and sat on his haunches, hushed and listening.

Tanaquil also felt the power of the music, which gentled her out of fear and stirred not her ears but her feet, until they began to prickle as if they would like to dance or run or splash in the surf. She ran to the oaken gate, raised the latch, and stepped into the street.

At first she was disappointed. Expecting a parade, she saw a single cart, wooden, with large stone wheels and green canopy, and drawn by an old, mottled, and mangy bear with a patch over one of his eyes. In the cart rode the flutist, a young man who, in order to play with both hands, had dropped the reins at his side. Fortunately, the bear seemed to know where he was going and indeed looked much too stubborn to be guided anywhere he did not wish to go.

Such a merry youth! His fox-red hair was adrift with wind, his oval eyes were the green of young acorns—she could see their color even from the gate. And what a tune he piped! Big, freckled fingers danced rapidly over the twin shafts which joined before they met his lips. His hair looked as if a tousled fox cub had crawled onto his head and fallen asleep. A rustic he seemed, and yet a god, a young Aristaeus straight from his beehives and his vineyards, who had come to town piping airs of the field and the forest. He wore not a loincloth but a shaggy green tunic, which enveloped his not very tall body rather like an unkempt bush. A homemade tunic for sure, muddied here, raveled there; just such a tunic as a country god, not one of the great celestials, might stitch for himself without a goddess to help him, and wash now and then in a muddy mountain stream. Last of all, she noticed his little feet, girl's feet almost, which were cumbered with sandals much too big for them, as if he hoped to disguise their littleness.

No longer did the bear look decrepit. His master's music seemed to be taking years from his back. Clippity-clop went his paws as he lifted them high in the air like the hooves of a horse performing in an Etruscan circus. Such a beast, of course, drawing such a musician, had inevitably attracted children, who paraded behind the cart like the fabled pygmies on their way to fight the cranes. A small, bow-legged girl, dressed in a piece of fisherman's net, attempted to hitch a ride and almost lost her balance. Dropping his flute, the flutist pulled her to safety and ensconced her at his side. She took the reins, snapped them vigorously, received a disdainful backward look from the bear, and settled into being a contented passenger and flaunting her preeminence over her friends on foot.

As the cart and procession vanished down the street, the flutist looked over his shoulder and sighted Vel; between pipings, he smiled. It was the kind of smile which made you want to spring onto the cart beside him, and Tanaquil thought wistfully, *He could have smiled at me; I was looking right at him.*

The smile, however, was not wasted on Vel, who leaped from the wall and loped after the cart.

"Vel!" Tanaquil called. Did he hope to follow the flutist out of the town? On the back of his hand he bore the brand of a slave, a crimson ring like the link of a chain, and no gatekeeper would allow him to pass without his master. Nor could he hide for long in Sutrium. Captured, he might be whipped or even executed by being tied to a corpse and thrown in a field to starve and rot. She thought of running after him. No, she decided. He was much too bright to attempt an escape. He would surely come back to the house when he tired of the music.

She closed the gate and returned to her bench. The honey of afternoon lingered in the garden, but as soon as she shut her eyes and tried to dream, she saw not the sunlight of imagination but the dark, shadowing wings of Vanth, the lady of death. Two years ago in Spina she had met the goddess and fled from her into the shadowless avenues of her dream. But Vanth was known to be grave, courteous, and very patient.

Vel returned in an hour. Tanaquil heard him from her room. She lay on a couch beneath a rock-cut wall where scarlet poppies whirled in a mural of mythological beasts: a horse with the spots of a leopard, a dog with the face of a cat, a lion with a tail like a two-headed serpent. She heard her father talking to him in the atrium.

Scolding him? No, his voice was loud but kind. In the middle of the afternoon, even slaves enjoyed a measure of freedom, and there was no reason why Vel should not have followed the musician. In fact, it sounded as if the musician had returned with him. At least she heard an unfamiliar and pleasantly rustic voice. She stirred from the couch, pausing to look at herself in a mirror of polished bronze and to smooth her hair with a comb of ivory. Bast, coiled on a smaller couch exactly suited to his long, lean dimensions, watched his mistress with golden indolence.

"Bast," she smiled "You have caught your mistress in a moment of vanity. But we have a guest—"

With a flush of confidence inspired by the mirror, and making a valiant effort to walk instead of run, she followed the hallway to the atrium.

She found her father attended by Vel and talking to the flutish, whose bee-swarm of freckles, she noticed, extended even to his feet. She did not acknowledge either Vel or his friend, but addressed her father with the nervous enthusiasm of one who, confronted by two young men and caught at a loss for words, solves her dilemma by addressing an older man. But even while she talked to her father, she watched Vel watching the flutist with a proud, proprietary eye, and she wished that this lecherous rascal of a Water Sprite were watching *her* with such an eye. Had her mirror not told her that she was—well, pleasing? Having given no thought to beauty for seventeen years, she suddenly felt impatient for men to confirm the image in her mirror.

Vel looked warm from his chase, and Tanaquil

wanted to say to him, "Vel, you are tired. Cool your feet in the pool." Could anything be more heartless than to keep a Water Sprite away from his lake? Homesickness, no doubt, was the whole explanation for his cruelty to dragonflies—and girls. A vision came to her of a gracious Tanaquil leading a grateful Vel back to his lake; Tanaquil serene with poppies and Vel in a decorous tunic.

Her father spoke. "My dear, the lad's name is Arnth." (*Lad!* she thought. *Why, he must be twenty-two*) "He's a histrion, a traveling player, and he has no place to spend the night. Vel has offered to make him a bed in the slaves' quarters. In return, he has promised to play for us after dinner."

How typical of her father to remind the young man that he was a traveling player, who must sing for his supper and then bed with the slaves! She was learning to resent the notion that every man, from birth to death and even into the Underworld, must keep his allotted station of slave, musician, farmer, soldier, or prince. Even Tarquin Priscus, it was said, before he emigrated to Rome and became the king, was scorned in Etruria because his father had been a Greek slave.

Ignoring her father, she addressed herself directly to the flutist. "If you don't wish to play, you will *still* be our honored guest."

Lars Velcha stiffened at his daughter's implied rebuke. Before he could speak, however, Arnth said:

"Playing is my job. It is also my pleasure." But he flashed a grateful smile to Tanaquil. (*At last,* she thought, *he has smiled at me.*) "Now, I must see to my bear."

"Vel," said Lars, "see that the bear is taken to the stable. Mind you, though, don't let him eat the horses." Then, with a bland, patronizing nod, he withdrew from the room.

The bear and cart waited beside the road. The bear, one of those huge, brown brutes which could kill a horse with the blow of a paw, glared at Tanaquil through his single good eye, as if to chide her for detaining his master.

"He bites," Arnth said, grinning without apology, and Tanaquil ducked into the protective embrace of the gate. The little spindly girl who had hitched a ride was still waiting in the cart. Rummaging under the canopy, Arnth found a honey cake, placed it in her hand, and sent her scurrying home. Then he unhitched the bear and patted the scruff of his neck.

"Ursus, will you go with our friend Vel? He's going to feed you and give you a place to sleep."

Invited instead of commanded, the animal followed Vel without protest.

"But I thought you said he bites," Tanaquil cried. "Won't he bite Vel?"

"Only women," said Arnth cheerfully. "He's a man's bear."

"Did you train him?"

"He's intelligent but untrainable. Ever since we took up with each other in the woods—that was four years ago—he's taken me on my travels. I'm not really his master. We travel together as friends."

"How did he get his patch?"

"He lost an eye in a fight with a wolf. He was very sensitive about it till he saw a circus horse with a patch. Nothing would do but I must get him one too. Now he's as vain of that patch as a woman with a new hair dye." He rummaged again in his cart and this time emerged with a basket of large, succulent figs ("For your slaves") and, of course, his flute.

"But where is your nightdress?" asked Tanaquil.

"I don't wear one."

"But how can you sleep in a tunic?"

"I don't. I sleep in the buff."

The image of Arnth in the buff, constellated with freckles, was so wickedly agreeable that she muttered to herself, "If he belonged to *me,* I would insist on a nightdress, as well as a change of clothes for tomorrow, to say nothing of a comb," though she had to admit that, in spite of his looking like an unkempt bush, he had an extraordinary freshness about him, a fragrance of holly leaves and wild thyme.

They reentered the gate. "Your house is like a big orange mushroom," he said. "It seems to grow right out of the earth."

"It does, in a way. Or right into the earth. My room is cut from rock."

The house was of wood and tile as well as rock. Wooden columns supported the walls, wooden beams the roof. But the walls were faced with tiles of orange terra cotta, and the tiled, gabled roof, flattened on top by a small, square platform to catch the rain, was as red as the sea when it drinks the setting sun.

They followed the roofless entrance hall to the atrium, which opened to further hallways on every side: to the west, connecting with the slaves' quarters; to the east, with the kitchen and pantries; to the north, with the triclinium for dining, the tablinum for study and conversation, and various smaller rooms for sleeping, bathing, and storage.

"Now," said Tanaquil. "You will want to rest and refresh yourself for tonight."

Lars Velcha and Tanaquil sat on sea-blue couches of citrus wood which swam with cushions like little white-capped waves. Beside each couch was drawn a table supported by three phallic Fauns; and three slaves, Vel among them, formed a continuous procession to and from the hallway which led to the atrium and thence to the kitchen, and heaped the tables with ewe cheese and ripe olives, sow's udder baked in tunny sauce, and venison smoked with silphium imported from Carthage. Pretending to wipe her fingers on a piece of bread, Tanaquil covertly watched Vel, who never raised his eyes from the rush-strewn floor. Though he seemed to be lost in thought, he glided among the tables with the ease of a cat; of Bast, for example, who had flowed under Tanaquil's table to wait, without impatience, for morsels spilled or dropped from his mistress' fingers.

Arnth did not appear for his performance until Lars and Tanaquil had ended their final course, a large honey cake in the form of a seahorse. Presumably he had eaten with the slaves in the kitchen. His earlier deference, however, had yielded to an actor's confidence. No longer a menial before a lord, he smiled at Lars and Tanaquil with perfect familiarity, paused until the slaves were out of the room and with them the clatter of feet and dishes, and announced a monologue about the Olympian gods. Tanaquil stopped him by raising her hand.

"Father," she said, slipping a piece of cake to Bast. "It was Vel who introduced us to Arnth. Can't he join us now?"

Lars smiled with paternal indulgence. "Certainly, my dear. I'm glad you're looking a little more kindly on the fellow. After all, it was for you I caught him." Black ringlets dangled along his forehead, like worms in a row, and his oiled, pointed beard looked sharp enough to puncture the skin of an apple. It was not surprising, thought Tanaquil that the enemies of the Etruscans called them the Sea Hawks. Proud and predatory they were, and yet at the same time the most affectionate parents in all the lands of the Great Green Sea. A Greek father looked upon his daughter as an unmitigated burden, to be married off as quickly as possible and with the least dowry acceptable to the groom. An Etruscan father looked upon his daughter as a good companion whom he gave in marriage with the greatest reluctance.

He clapped his hands and Vel appeared from the kitchen.

"Vel, my daughter has requested your presence. Stand in the door, if you like, while your friend performs."

Arnth's performance was more than a monologue. It was a dialogue in which he took all of the parts and accompanied them with gestures of hands and body or notes on his flute. The story concerned the blacksmith god Sethlans, whom the Greeks called Hephaestus, and how he had made a net to capture his faithless wife Turan (Aphrodite) in the arms of her lover Maris (Ares). Catching them in the very act of love, he summoned the other gods to observe their shame. Up to the moment of their capture, Arnth recounted the familiar story without embellishments. But no Etruscan could tell a Greek myth without a change, an addition or subtraction to make it livelier and usually naughtier, and Arnth's addition declared that when Turan and Maris discovered their audience, they smiled brazenly and performed in the net with a skill both nimble and abondoned. The gods who had come to mock ended by applauding, Sethlans was laughed from the room, and everyone agreed that any man was lucky to have such a beautiful and resourceful wife.

Arnth omitted no gesture or detail to convey his story. Now he was Sethlans, canny and vengeful; now Turan, shameless and irresistible; now Maris lover as well as warrior. But he kept his highest artistry for the last. When he reached the climax of his bawdy tale, he mimicked the very motion of the love act and tootled happily on his flute.

Lars was hugely amused. He slapped his knee and the black ringlets quivered like shaken worms above his forehead. Tanaquil was hugely indignant. *He's a Fescennine singer,* she thought. *A shameless rascal whose place is a low tavern or an army barracks. And it does not trouble my father that his virginal daughter should be submitted to such obscenities!*

She rose stonily on her couch and thrust a foot to the floor with the expectation of stalking from the room. Then she caught Arnth's eye. Before making his appearance, he had tucked the shapeless tunic around his waist with a sash; he had tidied his hair. Now, he was smiling directly to Tanaquil, and his smile was anything but lecherous. He was an actor waiting for deserved applause. He had not attempted to shock her; only to amuse and entertain. To Etruscan men, even husbands, adultery was an indiscretion rather than a crime, and the adulterous gods were thought more laughable than indiscreet. With a suddenness which left her shaken, she realized that the true reason for her anger was neither Arnth nor the lusty gods, but her own unmaidenly desire. In a word, she had envied the goddess in the net.

She answered Arnth's smile and lifted her foot from the floor. In turn, he lifted his flute and began the tune which he had played in the afternoon. Forests were in it, brown with fawns and playful with bear cubs, and country roads which wound through blackberry thickets and wild hawthorn, and vineyards purpling with grapes and peppered with bees, and all the waters of the countryside— lakes, rivers, streams; gentle or turbulent, wizening into a trickle with the heat of summer or galloping down from the mountains with melting snow. At first he seemed to be playing only for her. Then, he was also playing for Vel, who had slithered out of the doorway and started to dance.

Lars raised his hand. Slaves did not dance without their master's permission.

"No," whispered Tanaquil. "Let him dance."

He seemed to have flowed into a tide of clear, buoyant wine. His webbed toes hardly touched the floor. His serpentine arms floated above his head. He sank in the feathery depths; he shot toward the surface like a startled pike; he slept and dreamed. The silver-dusted loins, the slim, copper-colored torso became a wavering candle under the sea.

A sinuous shape joined him on the floor. What oceanic jungle had spawned this curious beast, with his leopard spots and serpent throat and his black-hinged, lashing tail? What currents flung him into the upper sea, whirling, twisting, flashing his savage claws in the light of a candelabrum shaped like a sphinx?

"Bast," she whispered, hating the dance, the beautiful bestiality of the dancers.

Bast ignored her; Bast and the dancer heard no mortal sounds, but only the piping of the sweet musician: the sweet, inhuman music of pipes which birds had taught, thrush and nightingale and fiery-throated phoenix; and Pan, who had taught the birds.

The music died; the clear, sustaining wine, as if it had lost the moon which governed its flux, sank and dwindled and dried, and left the dancers drained on the ocean floor: Vel, crouched on his knees, head bent, eyes closed, arms at his sides and touching the floor; Bast beside him.

Arnth, sliding the flute in his sash, went to them and placed a hand on Vel's bowed head. With wordless gratitude—less for the gesture, it seemed, than for the music—Vel embraced his legs, worshiping him, the magic musician.

Arnth spoke without embarrassment, without condescension: "We make a good team, don't we, Vel?"

Tanaquil stepped from her couch, and, usurping the function of a slave, filled two cups from a flagon of wine and held them out to the flutist and the dancer.

"You have both earned them," she said, forcing herself to smile; wanting, with a strange, fierce ache, to be a part of their music, their trust, their comradeship.

Lars loomed tipsily above his couch. "Another mime!" he clamored. "Phaedra and Hippolytus? But they didn't do anything; did they? He wouldn't —or couldn't. Europa and the bull then—"

"Father, Arnth is tired," said Tanaquil with finality. "You forget, he played in the town before he came to us. He will drink his wine in the atrium and then retire."

Flushed by her boldness in standing up to her father, she turned to Vel. "Have you prepared a comfortable couch for him?"

Vel looked at her with venom. "In the slaves' quarters, there is only stwaw."

"Take the pillows from my couch here," she said and, turning from him before he could answer or Lars could demand another mime, she conducted Arnth into the atrium. Behind them, a linen hanging rustled into silence, and the hoarse voice of Lars, summoning a slave to conduct him to his bed, fell to a rasp of weariness.

"He suffers gout," she explained, "and drinking aggravates it. I usually help him to bed. But tonight—"

"Tonight he is drunk. He won't know the slave from his daughter. My own father had gout. He cured it by eating a boiled tree frog, touching the ground three times, and repeating, 'Let the earth keep my pain; let health remain in my feet.'"

But Tanaquil was not interested in the gout of fathers. She pointed Arnth to a couch beside the pool. In the light of a cat-shaped lamp, the frescoed walls glinted with fishermen in a boat; they were dropping weighted lines while a dolphin leaped beside them and birds, incredibly red and blue, fluttered above them.

"Your house is like out-of-doors," Arnth

said. "The birds on the wall might really be flying. Even your little shrine is like the ones you see at the crossroads in the country." He pointed to the shrine of the household gods, a small portable temple, constructed of bricks no larger than a robin's egg, which held the silver effigies of the Lar, the Genius, and Tages, the Divine Child. "It makes me feel like playing on my flute. It has been easy to play here."

"You've come a long way?" Her conventional question concealed a profound and growing interest. She half-expected him to say that he had come from Arcadia and the haunts of Pan and Aristaeus, those pranksome godlings of the countryside.

"From Tarquinia. Before that, Clusium."

"Where are you going?"

"In a circle," he laughed. "The point is, always to keep going. Never to stop long enough for—"

"For what?"

"For the net to drop."

"What do you mean by the net?"

"A town can become one very quickly. Or marriage."

She thought: *Many a woman must have wanted to marry him. And some women must have settled for less than marriage.*

She said, "Have you ever been caught in a net?"

"My grandmother was an Etruscan lady," he explained. "A young widow who lived in a villa near Felsina. She was raped by a Gaul, one of a raiding party who seized and burned her villa and left her, bruised and unconscious, in ruins. People tried to be kind when she bore the Gaul's son, but the child—my father—was born with red hair which in those parts branded him as a barbarian. It was hard for him in the towns. No one could quite forget his origin and people looked as if they expected him to commit a rape or a murder at any moment. As a young man he went to live in the country—married a rustic girl and became a farmer. The town he had come from had been a net. So was the farm, he found, where he had to fight off wolves and try to get along with rustics who forgave his red hair but held it against him that he had come from a town. I loved him. And my mother. But not the net. When they died in an earthquake six years ago, I deserted the farm—what was left of it—and took up with some traveling players who taught me what I know about miming. I was sixteen. Two years later they settled in a town, but gave me their best possession, a canopied wagon. Ever since I have traveled and played."

"And laughed," she said. "I will never forget your laugh. It's like the melting snow when it fills up a dry stream bed. It sings and booms at the same time."

He laughed. "I am happy when I'm moving."

"Happier than now?"

"I'm moving now. Meeting you. Every person is a strange country at first."

"And when she becomes familiar?"

"I move again, but take the look of her with me."

"What will you take of me?"

"The way you have of dreaming and then bursting out of the dream like a lamp from a dark wine cellar, all bright and shining"

"A memory is poor company," she said. "It's

like the pool in this atrium. Today it's full. Tomorrow it may be as dry as a riverbed in fall."

"I have my bear," he said defensively. "He's the best of company."

"He can't talk to you, can he?"

"You mean I need human love." He looked at her with something akin to fear in his acorn-green eyes; they were oval eyes and not almond-shaped like those of most Etruscans. But then, his grandfather had been a Gaul. "Did you know that hunters have a net so fine that they can roll it into a ball no larger than an apple? But when they unfold it, it can hold a wild boar. That's human love. A finespun net which is quite inescapable."

"I know what you mean," she admitted, feeling as if she had lectured him to the point of rudeness, and now it was time to agree. "You don't even know when the net has fallen. Not till the strands cut you around the neck."

"Yes," he said. "And the goddess Turan ties up the ends."

"That was why you sang about *her* getting caught in a net. To get even with her."

"Yes. But of course I had to let her make the best of it. After all, she is a goddess."

"She'll still be angry with you. For getting her trapped at all."

"There's a worse net than love." he said. "There's slavery. That poor slave of yours, Vel. How did your father happen to catch him?"

She told him briefly and yet with a warmth which surprised her and sent prickles running up and down her back like baby squirrels. It was strangely pleasant, she found, to speak of Vel. She did not mention his behavior in the garden. In fact she had shut the incident into a nook of her mind, as a woman, fresh from the market with new purchases, may crowd an old pair of sandals into a chest.

"You are wrong to keep him."

"He belongs to my father. What can I do?"

He thought before he spoke. "Nothing, I expect. But someone else might help him. Someone who wouldn't have to stay around to face your father's anger."

"You realize that Vel isn't one of us. I don't think his feelings are quite human." At the risk of sounding heartless, she had to warn him. The garden incident, it seemed, could not be left in its nook.

"Neither are Ursus' feelings. They're ursine. But he feels all the same."

"I mean, even if someone should help Vel, he might not be grateful. He might be—hurtful."

"Vel?" laughed Arnth. "Why, he's little more than a child. Did you see how he crouched at my feet? A puppy looking for warmth."

She touched his hand, his big-knuckled hand with its fine sprinkling of freckles; touched the innocence of him and felt that at seventeen she was older in some ways than Arnth at twenty-two. At least she knew that Vel was not a child.

"Perhaps," she said slowly. "Perhaps someone will help him." She knew, of course, that she was acquiescing in Vel's escape, but whether she wished to free him or to be free of him, she could not say.

III

IT WAS NOT a squalid room by any means, Arnth saw. Etruscans did not build squalidly even for their slaves. The walls were painted with reeds and water fowl, dimly visible in the light of the crescent-shaped lamp which hung, moonlike, above the door. A window admitted the breezes of the night, pungent from the vineyards around the city, the grain mills and olive presses. But even a large room grows cramped when a dozen pallets are spread on the floor. He twisted his way among the reclining slaves—they looked like bodies after a battle, scattered at random—and found the pallet which Vel had reserved for him. Vel smiled happily and pointed to the cushions from Tanaquil's couch.

"Yours is the best," he said. "You will sleep like a swallow in its nest." As always, he spoke in Latin, and Arnth answered him in the same tongue:

"Not yet. I want to talk to you." He motioned Vel to follow him out of the room.

In the atrium, Vel looked furtive and frightened. The least sound would have startled him into flight. At this late hour, slaves were expected to sleep. The fins at his temples quivered, antenna-like, as if to alert him of dangers missed by his ears and eyes.

They sat on the bench which Arnth had shared with Tanaquil. He looked at Vel in the glow of the cat-shaped lamp, still burning fitfully, and wondered how Tanaquil could have thought him dangerous, this frightened lake-boy caged in a town and a house. Tenderness flooded him like warm olive oil. He could resist anyone except the weak and the helpless.

He whispered: "Can the hall porter hear us?"

Vel smiled. "Not unless he wakes up. He has learned to lean against the door and sleep on his stool." Except when he lisped, his Latin was measured and stately. He spoke without contractions.

"I'm going to help you back to your lake," said Arnth.

Vel looked at him with surprise. "Help me?" he said suspiciously. His eyes, yellow and faintly slanted, shone with their own light. "I am only a slave. Why should you help me?"

"And I am only a player. But you would help me, wouldn't you?"

"If you played for me, I would."

"Well, you danced for *me*. Don't I owe you something in return?"

Vel's face brightened. "Yes," he said, "I did, did I not? If you help me, I can dance for you again!"

"And never serve any master in any town!"

Vel captured his hand. "Never," he cried, and licked Arnth's knuckles like a grateful puppy.

As unobtrusively as possible, Arnth rescued his hand from the feathery tongue and touched the boy's head, whose close-grown hair felt damp and mossy. "Tomorrow I will hide you in my wagon."

Vel sighed. "No. Sometimes they search the wagons at the gate. In case the countwy folk have stolen anything."

"They don't always search, do they? I'm willing to take a chance."

"If we were caught they would whip both of us. Perhaps bind us to corpses and leave us to wot in a field. No, you must not hide me." He paused. "But if you want to help me another way—"

"How?"

"Go to my fwiends on the lake and tell them where I am. No one saw me captured. No one has seen me since. I am not allowed in the stweets on the Ninth Day, when my people come to market. Tell Vegoia."

"How can she help you?"

"That is for her to say." He appeared to draw a web across his eyes, to dim their light and conceal whatever strategems flickered behind them. His eyes had become disquieting and curiously old, like the eyes in the images of the Egyptian cat goddess, Bast. But Arnth was fond of cats, and he could not blame a slave for keeping a secret. Secrecy was the one weapon of the weak.

"How shall I find Vegoia?"

Vel recovered his earnestness. "Enter the fowest by way of the Road. Leave the Road at the lightning-blackened oak twee which looks like the comb of a wooster. You will find a path which leads to the lake. *Do not leave the path.* If anyone twies to stop you, give my name. At the lake, turn to the wight and walk until you see the Town of Walking Towers. Ask for Vegoia. My fwiends will hurt you if you do not speak my name *at once*. They do not like Etwuscans. Even with wed hair."

"I'll leave in the morning."

Early the next morning, while Tanaquil and her father slept the silken sleep of aristocrats, Arnth rode on his mission, winding through cobbled streets behind a drowsy and disgruntled bear, and jiggling the undigested bread, olive oil, and cheese which Vel had brought him from the kitchen. Ursus was petulant at having been roused from a warm bed of straw. Deliberately, it seemed to Arnth, he bumped the wheels against the cobbles raised for the crossing of pedestrians. But Arnth was happy. He was on the road. True, he was going to miss both Vel and Tanaquil. He had thought of asking the boy, once he was free, to travel with him in the wagon—to dance for audiences while he, Arnth, played on his flute. No, he decided. A lake boy needed his lake. As for Tanaquil—well, he had liked her far too much to linger in Sutrium.

He had also liked her town. Where the newer towns—Marzabotto, Pompeii, Spina—were designed as regularly as a pyramid, venerable Sutrium hugged the irregular terrain, like a natural growth of earth-hugging mushrooms. Streets followed declivities and buildings clung to hillocks. How the Etruscans loved the colors of earth! Though they lived in towns, they found their hues in the ocher, sienna, and umber of river banks and hillsides. Browns, reds, and oranges shone in the plaster faces of their wooden-walled houses and the tiled facades of their wooden-beamed temples. Here, to the right, was the circular shrine of Tages, the Divine Child, with a circus of grinning demons on its roof. The god himself, a small, wise boy with gray hair to denote his ancient wisdom, crowned the highest pinnacle and received obeisance from the demons. And there, to the left, was the palace of the King, flanked by a loggia with small, squat columns, jaunty rather than kingly, and roofed with a garden of spilling honeysuckle.

The shops in the marketplace had yet to open. The canvas stalls were shut like morning glories. A few animals—a mule, a goat, a stray serval cat—drowsed fitfully between the columns of the stoa. A few people were adventuring into the streets. A merchant was hanging robes of Milesian linen on hooks in front of his shop. A young woman, abroad on questionable business, smiled to Arnth. Her blonde hair was dyed, teased, and frizzed in the latest style; she flaunted a gold tooth as if to advertise the skill of Etruscan dentists; and her kohl-darkened eyes were as saucy as her upturned slippers. Before beginning his journey, Arnth had exchanged his baggy green tunic for a brief loincloth, white with large green polka dots the color of his eyes, and he had perched a domed, leaf-green cap precariously on his head. The woman of questionable business ran her eyes so avidly from cap to polka dots that she seemed to be counting his freckles. He knew her look. "Linger," it said, but his feet said, "Go!" He smiled pleasantly and signaled Ursus to increase his pace; and the bear, observing the feminine nature of the provocation, produced a burst of speed.

At the southern gate to the town, the guard was amiable if sleepy. A little fellow with a big sword, he crept out of the watchtower like a rabbit clutching a carrot between his paws. At the drawbridge, however, which stood at the lower end of a tortuous ramp, the guard was both sleepy and dour. Arnth could easily have waded across the dwindled summer stream, but his cart required the lowering of the bridge. The guard insisted on a thorough search, muttering under his breath that only thieves left the town at such an hour—why, the cocks had hardly crowed!

Rumbling across the oaken planks of the bridge, Arnth looked over his shoulder at the town, Tanaquil's town, which orangely, jauntily enfolded the cliff, and thought: *It is time to travel. A few more days and I might have wanted to stay.*

In the morning mist the town seemed suspended above the lake like low-lying clouds. Then, before Arnth's eyes, sunlight cut through the mist and revealed the slender pilings which held the towers: circular towers, with walls of green-painted reeds and oval windows abrim with geraniums and pointed roofs of big water lily pads in overlapping rows. Long-legged birds, roseate-white with scarlet shoulders and black-edged wings, flapped gracelessly but fierily above the houses and perched, from time to time, on a single leg to observe the people with whom they lived in harmony. Flamingoes. Flame Birds.

Dugout canoes, geranium-red, darted as briskly as water bugs between the pilings, while swimmers festooned their prows with garlands of water lilies and music reverberated from house to house—the pipe of a flutist perched atop a roof, the molten trembling of an unseen lyre. There were neither children nor old people; only youths and maidens, young men and young women. One canoeist was piping forlornly on a flute and allowing his craft to drift with the current. A swimming nymph erupted in his path, seized a garland, and draped him around the neck. Gratefully he dropped his flute and pulled her into his craft for several frenzied kisses and a long, consummating embrace. Gay, idyllic, and amorous: here were Vel's people. Arnth liked them.

He had parked his bear and his wagon beside the Road. Ursus, free to fend for himself during his master's absence, had squinted reproaches at him when he entered the forest. But Arnth had mollified him with a promise of blackberries. Waving farewell from the tree with the rooster's comb, he had found the path to the lake without difficulty. No one had tried to stop him. He had met and frightened a small, tipsy-looking bear which had probably eaten fermented berries, but neither Centaurs nor Fauns had crossed the path. Now, emboldened by the ease with which he had reached the lake, he called out to the swimmers:

"Ho, there! I want to visit your town."

The splashing stopped. The swimmers sank with the quickness of frogs. The canoeists raised their paddles like weapons. As quickly, the heads reappeared; the paddles were lowered. A canoe, then a second, separated itself from the flotilla and began a meandering course in Arnth's direction.

He waded into the water between the pads of water lilies, as big around as the wheels of his wagon, and the truncated mud cones of flamingo nests, now deserted. He noticed with approval that the canoeists were young women of splendid and unself-conscious nudity. In fact, they had started to wave with what could only be called an invitation.

The canoes bore down on him like frolicsome red dolphins. He opened his mouth to announce that Vel had sent him. He was not allowed to complete his announcement. Something captured his ankle and, squid-like, snaked him into the depths. It seemed that some of the boys had swum underwater ahead of the girls' canoes. He felt the domed hat fly from his head. Water invaded his lungs. . . .

His own coughing awoke him. He lay on his stomach. His hands were tied to his feet behind his back. He looked, he supposed, like an acrobat contorted into a ring, but he felt like a wheel supporting a heavy chariot. Grinning Water Sprites surrounded him—slender boys like Vel, girls with boyish flanks and piquant though modestly proportioned breasts. Both boys and girls exhibited the same pointed ears, the silvery down of fur against copper skin, and the slanted, feline eyes. Before he could finish his observations, he was jerked from the floor by his joined hands and feet and swung over an opening into the lake.

"Vel sent me." He gasped just as whatever apparatus supported him—a boom of sorts—dropped him into the lake. Water slapped at his face; he expelled his breath to protect his nose. Much more slowly than they had lowered him—reluctantly, it seemed—the sprites raised and swung him back over the reeds and dropped him none too gently to the floor.

"*Who* sent you?" demanded the boy in charge of the boom. His left ear looked as if it had been nibbled by a fish. He was wearing Arnth's hat.

"Vel," he gasped. "To find Vegoia." Inverted and waterlogged, he found phrases difficult and sentences impossible.

"Where is he?"

"Sutrium. A slave."

The boy looked undecided.

One of his friends lisped: "He is lying. Go on and dwown him. Everybody is *waiting*." To emphasize everybody's impatience, he prodded Arnth with a paddle. "Hard like a wock. Most of them have soft bellies."

"Get Vegoia," sighed the boy with the nibbled ear.

Vegoia was not long in arriving. A splash announced her emergence from the lake, and a ladder groaned with her ascent. Staring sidelong from his upturned position, Arnth saw that she looked about fifteen: a singularly knowing fifteen. Her body had the svelte lines of an otter, and her breasts were hard and exquisitely tipped with strawberry-colored nipples. Though her feet were webbed like Vel's, she walked soundlessly, and her eyes, though yellow and slanted, were those of a playful kitten instead of a cat. She was not human, of course, but what she lacked in humanity she more than compensated for in unabashed and glowing animality. While in build and coloring she resembled the other nymphs, she surpassed them in a quality which he could only call radiance: her honeyed skin, her hair the color of a spider's web in sunlight, and her smile, which totally lacked innocence but also guile and coyness.

With a slightly imperious nod, she dismissed her friends from the room; she seemed to occupy a position of authority. They lisped and grumbled at being deprived of a drowning, and the boy with the nibbled ear insisted that she recall them if the prisoner had not after all been sent by Vel.

"You must not keep him for yourself, Vegoia," he pouted, tilting his hat—Arnth's hat—to a rakish angle. "That would be gweedy."

Alone in the room with Arnth, she smiled. "Tell Vegoia about Vel." The nymphs, it seemed, though they lacked the lisp of the males, often referred to themselves in the third person.

"Unhook me," he choked, smiling back at her in spite of his awkard inversion. She released him from the boom, which seemed intended for raising canoes, and unbound his hands. His numbed members throbbed into pain. He gasped in spite of himself, and Vegoia, kneeling beside him, massaged his wrists and ankles with quick little fingers which drew his pain like a soothing plaster of mud and aniseed. It never occurred to him, an Etruscan male with a dash of Gaul, and a farm boy at that, to be embarrassed by his nakedness.

He told her about Vel. She listened attentively, then angrily. When he mentioned the crowded room which Vel must share with eleven other slaves, she cried, "They will smother the boy. He hates to be caged." And when he had finished, she growled, "May Tinia blast that town with a thunderbolt. Or," she added, "maybe Vegoia will."

"He said you could help him."

"Yes, She will bring him the cat's-eyes—" Her pause was ominous.

"Cat's-eyes?"

She ignored his question. "Vegoia will go to him tomorrow. On the Ninth Day, as you know, her people are allowed in the town. Now, she shall take you to her house. This, you see, is the council chamber. Shall she get a canoe for you?"

He said gallantly, shaking the water from one of

his ears: "I suppose I can swim."

"Follow Vegoia," She dove into the water, and Arnth, still a trifle liquefied, cautiously followed her by means of the rope ladder. He saw that she used her arms like fins and swam with a deft wriggling of her entire body.

Then he lost her. Dismayed, he searched for ripples to mark the place of her dive. The water around him lay as smooth and unwrinkled as a goddess in repose.

At a distance, the lake was less tranquil. A Water Sprite, identical for all he could see with Vegoia, waved furiously from her canoe and paddled in his direction, as if she intended to offer him a ride or run him down (one never knew with a sprite).

"Vegoia?" he called, blinking his water-reddened eyes and wondering if she had found a canoe for him after all. Or was this a stranger? From a distance they all looked alike!

Indeed, it was not Vegoia. "Begoe!" she shrilled, and swung at him with her oar.

He dove like a duck but not before Begoe's oar had smacked his bottom. Surfacing at what he hoped was a safe distance, he prepared to swim for his life, or at least his health, but Begoe chose to ignore him and pursue her business in other directions.

But where was Vegoia?

She rose at his side, spluttering with laughter. "Vegoia watched everything from underwater! Your bottom is as red as your hair. Come now; she will protect you from Begoe."

They approached a house which stood to the other houses as Vegoia to the other nymphs:

shapelier, brighter, prettier. A weary Arnth followed her up a wooden ladder through the inevitable opening in the floor—the Port·it was called. The interior, with its single undivided room, proved small but charming. A railing of dried grapevines, entwined with fresh honeysuckle, ringed the Port. A lyre of tortoise shell hung from the reed-and-wattle wall. A hammock woven of rushes and painted to look like a dolphin, even to the small mischievous eyes, swung from the ceiling. There were willowy chairs which seemed to be made from the tough stems of palm trees, and which, he found, accommodated his body far more willingly than did the stone benches in most Etruscan houses. A table of similar material held a sieve and a bowl of bucchero, a black Etruscan pottery which she had doubtless bought in Sutrium; and the bowl in turn held pomegranates and small cheeses shaped like fish. There were windows cut in the walls, their sills ablaze with geraniums and redolent with an herb called cicely. The air was fresh and sweet, not only with the pungent herb but with Vegoia's body. She could hardly be perfumed after their swim. It must be an exhalation, he decided, a musky fragrance which quickened his already rapid heartbeat and gave him the feeling that he had drunk deeply of unmixed wine.

Vegoia pointed him to the hammock. "You are certain that Vel is safe for the moment? He will not try to escape on his own?"

"No. He said he would wait for you."

"Well, then. There is nothing Vegoia can do for him now." She joined him in the hammock as easily as a fish sliding into a net. He felt the wetness of her, the warmth; smelled that frank and irresistible scent of musk. He sat up and all but tossed her out of the hammock.

"But you are Vel's girl. . . . Aren't you?"

"Sometimes. But Vel is in Sutrium and, no doubt, pleasuring himself with the Tanaquil you mentioned."

"Oh no, not with Tanaquil. She wouldn't permit it."

"No? What is she, a Sapphist? Well, even if Vel were here, he would want Vegoia to give you your guest-rights."

There was something decidedly pleasant about the prospect of claiming his guest-rights. But he made it an inflexible rule never to accept the more compromising favors of young women, who, he had learned to his sorrow, held out a cornucopia with one hand and with the other, a net. If a girl became importunate—and many were fascinated by his red hair and freckles, the Gaul in him—he simply hit the road. He had hit the road for such reasons at least twenty times, Now, he tried to escape from the hammock, but Vegoia, it seemed, preferred him prone. No sooner had he eased her out of his arms than she returned to them, like water filling a basin.

"Perhaps you prefer those citified ladies with dyed hair and plucked eyelashes," she said with some asperity.

"Actually, I've always preferred the rustic type."

"Is it curves and voluptuousness you want? Breasts like Begoe's? An older woman, and lots of her?"

"Quantity leaves me cold."

"Then," she cried, "you *do* like Vegoia after all. You are just being shy!" She paused. "Unless you are a"—she approached the word with caution—"*eunuch*. Have you dedicated anything important to that dreadful goddess, Cybele?"

"No," he snapped. "I have never worshiped Cybele, and if I had, I would not have dedicated anything important to her."

"Arnth," she asked with scarcely concealed amusement, "are you a virgin?"

"Of *course* not," he snorted. "You don't think that for twenty-two years, with all my travels—all the girls I've met, all the invitations I've had—in the towns, in the country—*everywhere*—that never once have I—" But how could he lie to those laughing, truth-divining eyes? "Yes," he sighed, like a small child admitting a theft of cookies. "I'm a virgin. But," he hurried to add, "only through choice. It's not that I don't know how. You might say, I know and forego."

Her laughter peeled like a tree full of thrushes. He was sure that all of her friends—the boy with the nibbled ear, Begoe, and the rest—could hear her, and it seemed to him that everyone in the town must suspect what had prompted her to laugh.

"Vegoia's first virgin," she mused and, crouching above him rather like a watchful cat, unsure of its perch, subjected his body to a hard scrutiny. "Well, she does not see any ill effects *yet*. But it is getting late, you know."

He tried to bury himself in the furthest folds of the hammock, to escape her scrutinizing eyes. She patted his shoulder, where four small freckles curved in a crescent.

"Listen," she said. "Eyes are useless unless you see with them, are they not? Ears are made for listening. Tongues for talking. Legs for walking. Every member has its purpose, useful or pleasurable. If you fail to use it, what happens?"

"It atrophies."

"Exactly."

It was time to explain his philosophy. "Everyone knows that women exact a price for their favors. They can't help it—it's the way they're made. In the marketplace or in the bedroom, they're always making bargains. That's their privilege. As for me, I'm too poor to pay in coins and too free to pay with my liberty. I travel. I intend to keep on traveling. In a word, I don't buy."

She dismissed his argument with a sniff. "You are used to Etruscan girls. Or Roman perhaps, those raw-boned virgins who scream rape if a man so much as winks an eye. Who is that ox all the fuss has been about lately? Lucretia, I think she is called. Here on the lake, we are not so serious about everything. If Vegoia gives you her hospitality, she is acting the part of a gracious hostess, nothing more. If you enjoy her, so much the better. Perhaps you will return. Perhaps not. But *marriage*. Why, we hardly know the word in the Town of Walking Towers."

He had to admit the strength of her arguments. "But what about love?" he asked desperately. "That's more binding than marriage. There's always the danger that gracious hospitality will tempt a guest into overstaying his welcome"

She looked at him almost wistfully. "Love," she mused. "Vegoia has heard about love, but does it really exist? Or is it a word you Etruscans made up to use in place of copulate? You are so fastidious. You do everything we do but call it by prettier names."

"What do you feel for Vel?"

"Vegoia does not love Vel. She likes him. He plays with her. Swims, fishes, sleeps. She likes the feel of his arms around her like grapevines, and the way his eyes shine in the dark and never leave her body. She likes the *zest* of him. She is going to help him but not because of love. Now then, have you talked enough for one day? Vegoia is not a conversationalist."

"I have your word then? No consequences—tears, promises, nets?"

"Vegoia swears."

"You realize that I am inexperienced in these things. Coming after Vel, I may prove a disappointment."

"Inexperience," she said, "can be a novelty. You have the wherewithal, and that is what matters."

He found, as he had long suspected, that he was an exceptionally hot-blooded and lusty young man, and therefore a dexterous pupil for Vegoia's instruction. To his instructress he brought the wherewithal of firm young limbs—of legs hardened by walks in the forest; arms which had pulled a plow and swung a sword; thighs as strong and limber as the trunk of a young maple tree—and turned their strength to a new, difficult, and delightful test of prowess, as if his body had become a bow, taut to eject its arrows. Hesitant at first, fearful of hurting, now he gains confidence, striving toward mastery, wanting desperately to please as he is being pleased, to imitate the gods who frolic in his songs and mimes!

In return, Vegoia imitates a young pantheress, a fury of grace and motion. Far from lying quiescent in his arms, she matches his passion with hands like wind-devils whirling across his body, as if to pluck his sinews, his freckles, the fine red hair on his chest and arms, to grasp and devour the manly savors of him. Her mouth is as sweetly avaricious as that of Turan when she devours her lover, Maris, in Sethlans' net.

And yet, what a curious thing! She has no pulse to answer his own furiously agitated heart. She is—heartless. . . .

He lay with her in the mute aftermath of love. He could not restrain a quiet little laugh of contentment and, yes, satisfaction. What man could? In spite of his inexperience, he had not proved inadequate. Might he not even call himself a distinct success rather than a mere adequacy? He began to calculate: *If I had begun at twelve like the usual farm boy, I would have enjoyed ten long years in which to improve my skills!*

At any rate, he need no longer celebrate the affairs of the gods. He could celebrate himself and Vegoia. It was as if he had taken his first swim in the sea when the waves were boisterous after a storm, and then eaten his first meal—breast of pheasant, pomegranates, and venison, all of his favorites—and drunk his first wine, a savory muscatel. Surprisingly, though, his hunger was not yet appeased.

"Vegoia," he whispered, "have you exhausted your hospitality?"

She opened her eyes. She glared at him with red and tearful anger.

"Vegoia!" he cried. "What's the matter?" I must have hurt her, he thought. Underestimated the savagery of my passion!

"You were laughing," she said. "I heard you. Just then!" (Vaguely he noticed that she spoke of herself in the first person: "I" instead of "Vegoia.")

"Because you pleased me so much. And because I hoped I had pleased you. Was I mistaken, Vegoia?"

"Is pleasure all you can talk about? After such a solemn and beautiful thing?"

"But you said—"

"I know what I said. But I was thinking of Vel and the other sprites. With you, it was different. You were so earnest and gentle." (Gentle! He had thought himself positively unbridled!) "Your eyes stared down at me like questing moons and—promised me things."

"They didn't know what they were promising," he muttered.

"What?"

"Nothing. I was just breathing heavily."

"And another thing," she cried. "I have started to speak of myself with familiar address. And you did not even notice!"

"I did notice but I didn't know what it meant."

"That I had honored you with my favors. What else?"

"How should I have acknowledged your, er—favors?"

"By respectful silence. Or, if you *had* to talk, by little intimate compliments whispered in my ear. *At the very least.*"

He had met her again, it seemed, the eternal

woman driving her eternal bargain, demanding payment for her so-called gift. It would not surprise him if her friends arrived to enforce a wedding.

"Oh, you *are* a beast, like all the Etruscans. You come into the forest, and I befriend you and save your life and then you seduce me and expect to ride off into the woods and leave me forsaken. I *know* you have had other women. I know you have. You were not a virgin at all. You are an experienced lecher, and I am just one of your conquests."

She sprang from the hammock, giving it a violent push and spilling him onto the floor. Before he could get to his feet, she dove into the Port and vanished with a splash which drenched the ring of honeysuckle and left the flowers askew and bedraggled. He considered giving chase but decided that, in her present mood, she would probably drown him. He selected a ripe pomegranate from the table—several were hard and several were starting to rot—and sat down in a wicker chair to ponder the vagaries of a Water Sprite's heart. Well, whatever they had in place of a heart. It was not long until he fell asleep.

IV

SPLAT!

A heavy, rotten object collided with his face and licked down his cheeks and chest. He blinked oozily to clear his eyes and saw Vegoia beside the table and brandishing a second pomegranate. He lunged backward so abruptly that he overturned his chair and sprawled onto the floor with a thud which shook the house.

Temple-bells of laughter agitated the room. "You look like a burst melon," she said, looming above him with another missile poised for descent. "It is hard to tell the seeds from the freckles."

"I don't need more of either," he said, in a voice which he hoped was subdued enough to antagonize her but strong enough not to sound plaintive.

She tossed the second pomegranate into the Port. It struck squashily and disintegrated on impact.

"Come now," she said. "Give me your hand. I promise not to drop you."

Restored to his feet, he faced her with wary expectation, rather like a convict in the arena as he waits to fight a trained dog.

"When I saw you sleeping—sleeping, mind you, after *everything*—and looking like a satisfied country boy who had just stolen a pig, I could not resist the pomegranate. It was rotten anyway. It was not as if I were wasting it." But her mood, he observed, was whimsical rather than recriminatory. Either she had forgiven him or she was feigning forgiveness with a poise which would have done credit to a lady of worldly Corinth or wicked Sybaris. "Take a dip now and clean yourself off, and I will fix your supper."

He dove through the Port and, paddling out from under Vegoia's house, cleansed himself of the fruit. He saw that most of the sprites had retired to their houses. Smoke curled from the roofs and brought to his nose the aromatic scents of supper. He was not long in climbing the ladder.

Vegoia had kindled a fire in a small oven. Assorted mussels, caught no doubt in the lake, browned on the shelf like diminutive bathers stretched in the sun. And a round loaf of bread, elephant-sized in contrast to the mussels, vied with them for the heat.

It was then that he saw Vegoia's company, a bird-like creature fluttering around the oven and looking, for all the world, as if he had come to supervise the meal. On closer scrutiny, Arnth recognized a Corn Sprite, one of those sylvan beings who helped the bees to scatter pollen and fertilize the crops. Grateful farmers repaid them with pots of honey suspended from olive trees. If you rode through the country around Sutrium, you could see the sprites by the dozen as they filled their cheeks from the pots and flitted back to their town in the forest. In spite of their size and gold, black-tipped wings, they were vaguely human in their faces and pink-skinned bodies.

Vegoia said simply: "This is Arnza. He has come to have supper with us."

Arnth smiled to Arnza, who acknowledged the smile with a slight dip of his head and continued to flutter helpfully above the oven, as if, by sniffing the smoke, he could gauge the time required to bake the mussels and bread.

"Pasta," Vegoia explained, pointing to the loaf. "Wheat grains and honeyed wine. When Arnza dips, I will know it is done. You see, it was he who gave me the recipe."

Arnth beamed his approval of Arnza's recipe. A day of exceptionally strenuous activities had whetted his appetite. He sat down in the chair which he had recently overturned and watched the preparations. It occurred to him to ask if he could help. Bachelor that he was, he was used to preparing meals for himself and Ursus. But he knew how women liked to wait on a man, to coddle and baby him and feed him delicacies from the kitchen. Far be it from him to interfere with an established domestic routine, especially since he was comfortable in the chair and, what with near drownings and hysterical outbursts, felt as if he deserved his measure of comfort. Anyway, Arnza was all the help she could use. What was the old adage? Too many cooks spoil the pasta.

She served him in a plate which was no more than the pad of a water lily with upturned edges. The mussels, browned and tenderized with olive oil, readily divulged their meat, which went with the bread like Castor with Pollux. The Corn Sprite, he noticed, did not partake of the bread, but lit on the back of his chair to observe his reaction, an oversolicitous cook eager for compliments.

For dessert Vegoia served some strong but not unpalatable cheeses.

"Sow's cheese," she said, and Arnth felt a bit lodge stubbornly in his throat and refuse to descend. But he managed to ease its course with a swallow of milk (cow's, he hoped), and decided that, all in all, he had rarely tasted a more satisfying meal. Inelegant, to be sure, but much to the taste of a rustic like himself.

As Vegoia served him, she moved with a lissome ease which was all the more provocative because (he assumed) she was not trying to provoke him. No longer the irate mistress, she had become, as it were, a graceful domestic waiting on a favored lord. He was charmed by her manner of walking, the way her webbed toes feathered along the floor, and most of all, the way her flanks looked trim and shapely from every angle, and not, as most women's, even young women's, like shapeless cauliflowers. Had the food been less alluring, he could not have taken his eyes off of her undulations. As it was, he alternated between large bites and lingering looks.

After they had finished—she and Arnza ate sparingly, but Arnth disposed of seventeen mussels, six cheeses, and the whole pasta—she threw the dishes into the Port and trusted the current to dispose of the scraps. On Arnth's plate, at least, there were only empty mussel shells.

"It is time for bed," she announced as casually as one might announce the temperature of a day in spring when it was neither hot nor cold.

The Corn Sprite took the hint. He flew at Vegoia as if he meant to attack her, but veered in time to avoid a collision, tapped her nose, and fluttered out of a window, pausing above a pot of cicely to sniff the air. Vegoia did not comment on his departure. She seemed to take it for granted that everyone received visits and culinary advice from Corn Sprites.

She occupied the hammock with the air of one who expects a joint occupation.

Since the sun had scarcely set, Arnth assumed that it was not sleep which she had in mind. This time, he hoped to avoid a repetition of tears and accusations. A few compliments and an earnest rather than a satisfied demeanor were a small enough price for the utmost in hospitality. With the solemn glide of a priest entering a temple, he moved to join her in the hammock.

But what was this? A knotted and stubborn fist did not exactly thump him in the chest, but it held him irresistibly at bay.

"But where am I to sleep?" he wailed.

"In the chair."

"A man can't sleep in a chair!"

"You did when you took your nap."

"But then I was tired. Now I'm refreshed."

"Try the floor. You may use your loincloth for a pillow. I got it back from my friends while you slept."

She returned the loincloth as if she were making him a princely gift, though the dye from the green polka dots had run and faded.

"And your hat." His hat had shrunk to the size of a sand dollar.

Making the prescribed pillow, he stretched on the floor and unrolled his not very long frame as if he were seven feet tall and each bare inch were intimidated by the reeds.

"You know," he sighed, "my skin is very fair and tender. It goes with my red hair. Gallic hair. Tomorrow I'll be a mass of welts."

"No one will notice them among your freckles."

It was almost dark now. Through a window he watched the lights flickering on in the other houses.

"Vegoia," he said. "In those other houses, are there several hammocks?"

"One to a house."

"But what if there are *two* people?"

"They share the hammock."

"Nobody sleeps on the floor?"

"Except Etruscans."

"Vegoia, will you fetch me a coverlet to put under my back?"

"Look in the chest."

"Which chest"

"The only chest."

"Where?"

"Behind the chair in which you turned over."

Obviously, she enjoyed reminding him of his mishap with the pomegranate. Was he mistaken or did she utter a low silvery laugh which merged with the laughter tinkling from the other houses and the other, cozier hammocks? Sighing, he rose and stumbled to the chest. He raised the heavy lid, rummaged among the contents—net, sandals, fishing spear —and found a coverlet, furry and rather odorous. Bear's pelt, he supposed. It helped to soften the floor, but the smell of bear was as rank as Ursus in the winter when he refused to bathe.

After a little while, he said: "Vegoia, I can't sleep."

"No?"

"There are lumps in the floor. And a draft." It was more a plea than a whine.

"You are a farm boy, are you not? You must have slept on the ground many times. When a frost threatened. When wolves were harrying your flocks."

"Never after such a hard day."

"But a little while ago you said you were refreshed."

"Not *that* refreshed. Besides . . . I'm lonesome."

"An old bachelor like you?"

"It was very upsetting being almost drowned today. My rescue has made me feel—well, convivial."

He heard her rise from the hammock and come, he hoped, to investigate his situation on the floor. He twisted himself into an attitude of pained endurance and followed the glow of her eyes through the dark. They moved toward him like astral bodies and then, directly above him, paused; a waterfall of fragrance fell to his nostrils. He sat up and reached vainly to catch her hand, like a tired swimmer who gropes for a raft and splashes it out of his reach. He heard the hammock receive her returning weight. Then, silence stifled the room, punctuated after a time by the cry of a night-jar, the low laughter rippling from the other houses, the murmur of water under the house.

"All right," she said at last. "You may share the hammock."

He bounded into the hammock and scooped her into his arms as an iron-tipped plow scoops a stubborn rock.

"Sleep, I said. Not visit. Early to bed, early to boat."

"I'm not sleepy."

"I am." She arranged herself in the crook of his arm, her head against his shoulder, her hair as soft as the fur of a cat, and rebuffed all efforts to kiss or fondle her.

"Are you really going to sleep?" he demanded.

"That is what I said."

"At least talk to me, Vegoia."

"My dear," she said, "what you mean is, 'Listen to me.' You have made love, you have eaten a large supper, and now, if I will not make love to you again, you want me to listen to you."

And of course he did. About his red-haired father, who loved the country but could never quite forget the rumble of chariots in the city, the blithe little temples painted like courtesans; and his mother, who had never learned to read scrolls or inscriptions, but who could interpret flashes of lightning and the entrails of a sheep and divine the will of the ancestral spirits which hovered, restless and sometimes malicious, at every threshold and envied the living their loves. Yes, he wanted to talk about himself and his dead parents, but he wanted equally to listen. Traveler, wanderer, player with flute and song, he had listened for six years to the voices of the forest, which spoke to each other but not to him; not, at any rate, to show that they recognized his identity as a youth and then a young man, hot-blooded, longing, and sometimes lost. Now, he wanted someone to answer him, longing for longing, lostness for lostness. What did he know about her? That she was as bright and pretty as a tiger moth; quick to love and to take offense; and highly skilled as a cook. He did not know her heart, or rather, what it meant for her to have no heart. He wanted—what was the word?—communion.

"Vegoia," he said. "Why don't you have a heart?"

She did not answer him at first. When she spoke, it was a thin wraith of a voice which made him think of her eyes and how they had shone in the dark and seemed to be disembodied.

"When the Builder made us—"

"Builder?" he said. "Do you mean Tinia?"

"Older than Tinia. The Power who made the gods, and then made men. When the gods die, the Builder will abide. It is said that he made us late in the fifth day, the fifth thousand years of creation, after he had tired himself with the birds and reptiles and mammals. Already he was thinking of the sixth day, when he must make man—thinking and saving his strength for his most difficult task. Thus, tired and preoccupied, he forgot to finish us; forgot to give us hearts. He thought of it later, of course. But already we moved and we spoke. It hardly seemed worth his while to discard us and try again. So he put us into the woods beside this lake and taught us to fish and swim, to build boats and eventually houses which seemed to walk on the water. In order to survive, we had not need for hearts. What good was a heart against a cave-bear or a tiger as big as an ox? And then, when the fiercer beasts were gone and it was not a question of survival but of being happy, we had the woods and the waters and our swift, beautiful bodies."

"At first, when there were few of us, we bore children to increase our numbers and fight our enemies. Then, not very long ago, we had no further need of children, and something changed in us. Our wombs forgot to swell. Our breasts ran dry of milk. Even now, some believe that the goddess Turan is punishing us for having made light of love. But never mind. We live long lives and keep our beauty almost to the last. Did you know that I am thirty? Yet in Sutrium, I am sometimes taken for a child. 'For shame,' a merchant once said to me. 'What do you want with carmine to stain your lips? Here is a ribbon to tie in your hair!' In a century or so, when I am old and withered, I shall go to the Great Mundus in the forest and join my ancestors. It is the way of my people. The old, the lame, the homely—they go of their own accord. We have no place for them in the Town of Walking Towers."

"And you never miss having a heart?"

"I think," she said, "that it is better to have no heart, than to have one and not to use it."

Early the next morning, Arnth and Vegoia paddled ashore and took the path to the Road. Some of the sprites had accompanied them in canoes and now, lingering on the bank, talked volubly of Vel's return and how they would deck his houseboat with flowers and make him forget his weeks of slavery. No one seemed to doubt Vegoia's success. Without exception, they showed her a subtle deference. It was not that she frightened or cowed them; rather, they seemed to be children deferring to a wise sister.

"But why aren't any of them coming with us?" Arnth asked. "This is their market day."

"Not today," she said, with cryptic brevity.

He was wearing his loincloth and his shrunken hat, and she, because of her mission in town, had donned a dapper tunic of fur which made a pretense of hiding her breasts. In her hand she carried a plate of hornbeam wood, raised at the edge, and around her neck she wore a bulla, a hollow sphere which opened on a spring and which rattled with stones or coins. He wanted to ask her about them—amulets were they, to ward off demons?—but her silence did not encourage questions.

Ursus was waiting for them beside the wagon. The burrs in his coat suggested adventures in the woods. He greeted them with his usual ominous growl.

"He doesn't like women," began Arnth, but Vegoia was already stroking his massive head. Ursus subsided into—for him—a benign mood and ceased to growl, though his single red eye and his rakish patch implied that a bear's benignity, this bear's at any rate, could be short-lived.

"He usually bites women," said Arnth with a trace of disappointment.

"Etruscan women," corrected Vegoia. "Not sprites, I think."

They were not alone on the Road. The woods, like black waves humping onto a beach, had begun to eject a curious flotsam of Weir Ones. A Centaur, old and halting, ambled past them in the direction of Sutrium.

"He is going to get himself shod." whispered Vegoia. "And there—do you see the Paniscus?" She pointed to a little hairy chap—horns, tail, cloven hooves—who was clutching a chunk of copper in his paw. "He will go to a depilator and have some of that hair removed from his tail. In the town, they use a mixture of pitch and dead frogs." One or two of the Weir Ones nodded to Vegoia; the others ignored her and, for that matter, ignored each other, unless of the same race, and Arnth concluded that the various tribes of Weir were staunchly, irritably independent except in their common disregard for the race of men.

"Get in," he said, pointing to his wagon. "I'll drive you to the gate. In fact, I might just drive you into the town. I would like to see Vel again."

"No." she said. "Not to the gate, and certainly not into the town. The guards would wonder if they saw you drive up with a Weir One. We are not supposed to like each other, you know."

"I can follow you in later."

"No," she repeated. "If we met in the streets you would give me away. Your eyes are so naked. They show everything."

"Then—we must say good-bye?" She was smiling to him; a little girl in a fur, with tow-colored hair which she had valiantly combed with a comb of tortoise shell but which the wind on the lake had shaken to a sweet wilderness. She might have been bound for market to buy ribbons for her hair. Yesterday he had desired her. Now, he pitied her—the slightness of her body, the childish air of confidence which seemed to ignore the danger of her mission. At the word "good-bye" sadness stuck in his throat like a twig.

"Arnth," she said, taking his hand. "I want to tell you something."

"Yes, Vegoia?"

"I forbid you to forget me."

He read in her smile the strength and authority which her people acknowledged with their quiet deference. It was as if the little girl had grown up before his eyes.

"I don't want to forget you."

"You want to. But you cannot. Any more than you can rid yourself of freckles."

"Vegoia," he cried. "There is something about you now. A difference. A power. You really can save Vel, can't you?"

"Yes."

"How can you be so sure?"

"Surely you know who I am!" she said with amazement. "Why Vel sent you to me!"

"Because you are his friend."

"Because I am the town's sorceress."

V

EVERY NINTH DAY, the market of Sutrium not only contained the bright canvas stalls of the local merchants, but the stone-wheeled wagons of farmers from the surrounding countryside; and finally, the lone, straggling figures of the Weir Ones, who owned neither stalls nor wagons, but wandered up and down the lanes with baskets under their paws, exchanging lumps of copper or fresh fish for the artifacts and services of the town. As always, Tanaquil walked the streets with absolute confidence and without the modest misgivings of a Grecian girl, who, if she visited a market at all, would have veiled her face and traveled with an escort of slaves. Tanaquil, in fact, welcomed the stares of the men to reassure her that she had dressed becomingly: a tunic of oakleaf-green which fell to her ankles; a silver mantle, embroidered with green seahorses; a multitude of bracelets jangling from wrist to elbow and flaunting Phoenician scarabs of deep blue smalt, entrapped by Egyptian lotus-leaves of fine-spun gold; and on her fingers, three ivory rings which coiled like olive leaves. In her hair, she wore her customary poppies, arranged in the shape of a fillet.

"Like scarlet hands," a household slave, Athenian and therefore eloquent, had said to her, "offering the blackness of your hair to the gods in sacrifice." (But Vel had said nothing; Vel, to whom she had smiled as she left the house.)

Inarticulate with shyness—they had not yet visited the wine shops—the Weir Ones lumbered between the stalls, stepping on outspread merchandise and wincing beneath the imprecations of angry merchants. A Centaur trod on a bunch of grapes and slid with a whinny onto his haunches. *Poor old beast,* she thought, *his hooves were never intended for cobbled streets.*

She scanned the faces and bodies of the Weir Ones, looking for silver hair and webbed feet. If Arnth had visited the Water Sprites as she suspected, perhaps Vel's countrymen were even now in the town, eager to help him return to the lake; to smuggle him through the gate, across the drawbridge, and into the forest. Odysseus himself would envy such a feat! *Suppose,* thought Tanaquil, *I myself conspired to help him escape. Suppose I should drive a carriage up to the gate, with Vel under the canopy!*

"Destination?" the guard would ask.

"Viterbo."

"What's in the carriage?"

A sweet, disarming smile. "Why, robes and slippers—and a basket of poppies."

"Pass"

Pass. To forest and lake. With Vel. A Vel whom gratitude had eased of carnal threats and cold indifference.

She approached a female Faun who was selling bouquets of flowers. Many a human woman had lost her heart—and more—to the mischievious charm and unabashed virility of a male, but never, as far as she knew, had a human man succumbed to a female. The one in question resembled a large quail, squat, squashed one could almost say, with hair everywhere, even on her chin. She wore a goatskin around her trunk, but what she needed was an ankle-length robe to hide her legs. Tanaquil handed her a gold coin, an *as,* and took in exchange a pathetic bunch of asphodels, whose blossoms in the country opened with sharp little cracks so that travelers sometimes thought themselves under attack by slings or blowguns. The blossoms presented to Tanaquil, however, by a fist like a big black spider, had long since opened and now seemed poised to close and wilt. Feeling affable and generous, she smiled to the woman, bade her a gracious good-bye, and looked for a child to whom she could give the flowers. Behind her, she heard in broken Latin:

"Fine lady with all them airs! Charun roast her soul!"

Her spirits dampened if not drowned, she skirted the stall of a depilator, who was toiling to rid a Paniscus of excess hair.

"More off the tail," the fellow chided. "But watch the tip, mind you. I want it to fluff."

And then she came on a girl whom she recognized instantly as one of Vel's people. A web-toed girl with a trim fur tunic—warm for summer, it looked, but flattering to her figure—and the prettiest heart-shaped face she had ever seen. Her skin had the smooth glaze of amber, the kind which came from the far northern river called the Danubius. She seemed to be demonstrating a trick, in return for which the watchers, five young swains who clearly preferred the magician to her magic, would drop some coins in a wooden plate which lay at her feet. There was also a circle of watching cats: big, glossy fellows with yellow fur and black spots. Cousins to Bast, but much less civilized, she would say. Closer to their African heritage.

Tanaquil saw that the girl had cast a spell on a certain young man with an ochre cloak. His eyes looked glazed; he stood as still and wooden as the figurehead of a becalmed ship. She was telling him to extend his hand. At first she spoke in Latin; the hand remained at his side. Not all Sutrii were bilingual, it seemed. Then, she spoke in Etruscan. Out shot the hand, open and trusting. Casually the girl removed from her tunic a fibula, a pin with a coral head, and drove it up to the head in the man's palm. He gave no sign of pain. The crowd suspected a trick.

One of the watchers, a youth with large feet which were housed in wooden sandals, cried: "You didn't really stick him, did you, Spritey?"

Smiling, the girl withdrew the point, which glistened with blood and left a small red wound, the size of a gnat, in the victim's palm. Tanaquil winced. The young swains cheered and filled the plate with gold, but shook their heads when asked if they cared to volunteer as subjects. The victim, awakened by a slap to his cheek, looked down ruefully at his palm and followed the others to the nearest wine shop.

But the cats lingered, drawing around the magician as if she had promised them a dinner of quails and cream. She knelt in their midst and held out a handful of small, greenly glittering jewels and seemed to address them. At any rate, her lips began to move, though Tanaquil could hear no words. The cats responded with frightening vehemence. Fur rose on their backs. They slashed the air with their tails. They snarled and hissed and tensed their long bodies. Then, before they could vent their ferocity, the girl dismissed them with a nod of her head. They neither slunk nor scurried, but strode with pride and arrogance, heads high on the tall necks, ebony spots flashing like black pearls.

Tanaquil shuddered. She had never seen Bast in such a mood. She felt as if she had intruded on an arcane ritual. It was best to announce her presence.

"Are you a sorceress?" she asked politely.

The girl looked at her with surprise. "Yes"

"From the lake?"

"Yes. The Town of Walking Towers." Her answers were brief but not unfriendly. She stared at the poppies in Tanaquil's hair.

"I think I know one of your people," Tanaquil continued. "Here in the town."

"None of my people live in Sutrium."

"This one is a slave. His name is Vel."

"And you must be Tanaquil?"

"Arnth sent you, didn't he? Where is he now?"

"I left him in the forest."

"Are you related to Vel?"

"I am his friend."

Friend? thought Tanaquil. *No, his woman.* Jealousy stung her like black henbane.

Vegoia took her hand. "His friend —like you. Together we shall help him. No?"

How small were Vegoia's fingers! A child's fingers, exigent, not to be denied, touching her heart as well as her hand; probing gentleness to the very roots of her being, like an antidote for the henbane of jealousy.

"People can watch us here," said Tanaquil. "You see the temple over there, the one with the statues on top—the demons and little Tages? It ought to be empty now; the priest goes to market like everyone else. I just saw him. Follow me there in a few seconds."

The temple to the child-god Tages perched on its platform like a big clay toy which was painted with all the colors of a rainbow: shell-orange for the tiles which covered the wooden walls—purple for the low triangle of pediment—and *every* color, green and black, lemon and blue and rose, for the grinning, prancing demons on the roof. It might have been painted by the god himself. Only a child, thought Tanaquil, Etruscan at that and very knowing, could have splashed his colors with such a disregard for Athenian harmony, and modeled such young, outrageous, and irresistible imps, who were bent on mischief even while they seemed to attend their master, Tages.

They were phallic imps, of course. Like Vel.

She climbed the tall steps and passed between the columns of the porch and into the cella or room of worship. She had to watch her step. The temple was a sanctuary for unwanted kittens. The priest fed them from the offerings and, once they were grown, found homes for them with Etruscan families. A little speckled fellow clung to her sandal and allowed himself to be ridden across the tiles of the floor. Tanaquil dislodged him with difficulty. Being a serval kitten, he had strong claws. Then she examined the room, which never failed to enchant her.

The walls were decorated, childishly and touchingly, with little boys climbing into chariots made of seashells, and a terra cotta statue of Tages, smaller than the one on the roof, stood on a pedestal and looked down at her with boyish roguery. He was clumsily done, to be sure. The Etruscans had yet to overtake the Greeks, who had learned, after centuries of stiff Egyptian frontality, to capture the natural grace of the human form. The eyes were exaggerated in their slant, the limbs were loose and awkwardly attached to the body. Nevertheless, he radiated life; in fact, he looked uncomfortable on his pedestal and as if he might clamber down on those loose limbs and ask—or demand—a ride in one of the shell chariots. Her own brother Aulus had also been a stocky, fearless, and energetic boy, and Tages had always been her favorite god. She loved him infinitely more than his quarrelsome grandparents, Tinia and Uni, or the bleak and sinister Vanth.

Vegoia followed her silently into the cella and stopped, marveling, beneath the statue; then, with affecting deference, she bent and kissed the sandaled feet of the god. *Really,* thought Tanaquil, *the girl is incapable of a false or awkward movement.* Anyone else would have looked as if she were parading her piety.

"And the pictures on the wall!" Vegoia cried. "Those dear little boys! They are going to race their chariots."

"They really do, you know. Right here in Sutrium. Once a year, the market is cleared of stalls, and the little boys hitch wagons to asses and race each other for the prize of a red cart with copper wheels."

"How I would love to see them race! Do they ever get hurt?"

"Never. Though sometimes they do get tummy aches from all the sweets fed to them after the race. But the boys on your lake must have races too—with boats."

"They did," said Vegoia. "So did Vel, once. But that was years ago. They have all grown up, and there is no one to take their place."

"No children at all?"

"It is not as if we really needed them," she said quickly. "We live for a very long time and when the last of us die—well, let the flamingoes have our lake. Now we must talk about Vel."

"You've come to help him escape?"

"Yes"

"What can I do?"

Vegoia looked at her searchingly, and Tanaquil felt as if the yellow eyes were probing into her heart; or perhaps even the soul which, she hoped, would survive the death of her body and dwell in the after-life of love, games, and banquetings. Vegoia's eyes looked immeasurably older than her slight girl's body. Not that they were tired; but they looked as if they could not be fooled.

Vegoia opened her bulla and drew several of her brilliantly green gems with yellow stripes. Cat's-eyes. Stones from the East reputed to possess powers as a talisman. The kittens, at least a score of them, began to press at her ankles.

"Give these to Vel," she said.

"He will know what to do?"

"Yes. Quickly now. Hide them under your cloak." She stooped to caress the kittens, one of which had clambered up the fur of her tunic.

"I'm glad you've come," said Tanaquil. "Vel has been caged for too long."

"You like him, Tanaquil?"

"Yes. Very much. Though I'm afraid of him too."

"I *told* Arnth that Vel would have his way with you."

Tanaquil flushed. "He has not had his way with me."

Vegoia looked skeptical. "And yet you say you like him."

"But I do!"

"Why deny him then? His pleasures are few, I think, in your father's house."

"He would have taken me without kindness."

"You are perhaps a virgin?"

"Yes."

Vegoia laughed. "Two in as many days."

"What do you mean?"

"Arnth."

"Arnth a virgin? But he sang such wicked songs. As if he understood *everything*."

"*Now* he understands."

Honestly, it looked as if every young man who crossed Tanaquil's path had been enjoyed by Vegoia. Not that anyone expected virginity in a man. In fact, Tanaquil had come to accept, even to savor the worldly image of Arnth. But to hear that he had been a virgin when she met him, and then lost his virginity to Vegoia—well, it seemed such a waste. Vegoia was not a girl to appreciate the rarity of his gift.

But she saw that Vegoia was not boasting. The nymph was speaking naturally about a matter which to her was very natural.

"I will take your stones to Vel," said Tanaquil.

Vegoia was looking at the pictures on the walls. "Have you ever wished, Tanaquil, that they always stayed like that? Little boys, mischievous but not really—wounding?"

"And not having to go away to fight wars and *be* wounded," said Tanaquil. "Yes, I certainly have."

"But they do grow up," said Vegoia. "And their boyish bodies harden to the sinews of a man, and they grow desirous and desirable as well as mischievous. But they keep their little boys' hearts. Quick. Merry. Forgetful." She turned from Tanaquil as if to study the pictures, gasped, and pressed a hand to her heart.

"You have a pain in your heart?"

She removed the hand and shrugged. "My heart? I have no heart. Like Vel."

Tanaquil was puzzled. "I don't think you are heartless at all. Either of you. Only wild. I think I could learn to be wild myself."

"Not in our way. Wild to you means living in the woods. Wearing a fur like mine—or nothing at all. Hunting, fishing, talking to the birds. Wild to us means— not caring. Go to Vel now. Take him the stones. But I think you were wise to deny him his way. Yes, he would surely have hurt you."

Vel, on his knees, was scrubbing the floor with fuller's earth. His movements were spry and quick, and the red tiles of the atrium glowed like embers in the slanting light from the roof. But he seemed bemused; as if the ladder of light could carry him out of the house. Another slave was working with him, the Athenian who had complimented Tanaquil's beauty: a minikin fellow with black, inquisitive eyes which looked as if they loved to spy secrets.

"Vel," said Tanaquil. "Come into the garden with me, will you?"

The Athenian stared at her as if he had just spied a secret; his eyes seemed round black olives sparkling with brine. Vel followed her at a distance; she could hear the slap, slap, slap of his feet.

In the garden there were no dragonflies, and no poppies in the mouth of the shrine to Lavis—Tanaquil had cut them for her hair. There was only Bast, asleep among the flowerless poppy stalks. Tomorrow, perhaps there would be no Vel to enter the garden with her. Now, she was not afraid of him. She had talked with Vegoia; she understood his wildness.

She opened her palm to display Vegoia's cat's-eyes.

"Vegoia has come!" he cried.

"Yes. I saw her in the marketplace. She told me to bring you the stones. That was all."

He snatched them out of her hand and clutched them jealously between his long, narrow fingers.

She waited for a word or a gesture of gratitude. "You will be going with her?"

"Yes"

"Can you tell me when?"

"Soon"

"Vel, you understand that I never meant you harm," She laid her hand on his moist shoulder.

He did not acknowledge the touch. "It was for you your father caught me."

"But I never told him to."

"It was for you." He pointed to the crimson ring on the back of his hand; the indelible brand of a slave.

She caught his hand and pressed it against her cheek. "Vel, Vel. May I come to visit you on the lake and meet your people? I liked Vegoia. Truly I did. I'm sure I will like the others. You see, I—I am very fond of you."

"Where is Arnth?" he asked. "He did not come with her, did he?"

She dropped his hand. "She left him in the forest."

"Arnth has no love for towns," Vel said proudly. "He will come to see me on the lake."

"And play for you? That's why you love him, isn't it? His music."

"Arnth *is* music." His face seemed a burst of sunlight. "When he plays, he is all a shining and a sweetness, and I want—"

"What?"

"To dance for him."

"And me?"

"You? You are a *woman*. What would I want except to—" He laughed and caught her wrists with vicious fingers: talons.

"No," she said. "First you must respect me. As you respect Arnth."

And then they heard Arnth's flute, and the big-wheeled cart, rumbling up the street.

Vel released her as if a scorpion had stung him. "You said—*he was safe in the forest.*"

VI

HE WATCHED HER, a small, resolute figure with a wooden bowl in her hand, follow the Road until she was lost in the company of Weir Ones—towering Centaurs, hairy Panisci—and hidden by the green meanderings of the trail. "The town's sorceress." Sorceress, he wondered, or little girl playing at spells and incantations? And yet there had always been a strangeness about her, an intimation of angers and anguishes which were anything but childlike. He had seen her wrath. He could guess her power.

Meanwhile, Ursus had grown impatient. He began to paw the ground and crackle the dry leaves.

"All right, Ursus," Arnth said softly. "It's time to go."

Harnessed at last, Ursus lifted his stalwart legs, which, rolling like water wheels, powered him into motion until he belabored the Road as if he were driving before the blast of the wind-god, Boreas. Going—where? Arnth did not know. Viterbo. Volsinii. Spina perhaps, and even one day the towns of the red-haired Gauls, his grandfather's people. Somewhere, anywhere, away from his three perplexing friends: the child who was thirty years old and had no heart; the web-toed boy whom she hoped to rescue with the help of sorceries; and the girl who inadvertently, like a dazed sleeper stumbling out of a cave, had crossed their path.

Vegoia, Vel, Tanaquil. Water Sprites and human girl. He saw their faces, like brilliant lilies against the green opacity of a pool. Which would remain afloat and which would drown, its petals shredded in the obliterating waters? Etruscans did not easily relinquish their slaves, and enslaved Weir Ones did not easily forgive their masters.

He knew, as suddenly and certainly as he had liked Vel and Tanaquil and desired Vegoia, that he must return to Sutrium. Return, help, heal. *Be* there, that was the thing.

He shouted, he jerked on the reins, he felt like Hippolytus in his runaway chariot; and then he waited. Ursus could not be hurried; first, he acknowledged Arnth's message with a growl of aggravation. Then, with a casualness which approached insolence, he slowed, paused, turned, and jogged toward Sutrium at the pace of a superannuated mule.

Once he had changed his course, Arnth was not in a hurry. He had no wish to overtake Vegoia on the Road and risk her wrath and even her sorceries. She had more reasons than one to punish him. Multiply the number of his freckles. Turn him into a fish or a bear or even an overripe pomegranate. Or, with peculiarly appropriate justice (so she would think), subtract him into a eunuch.

He sighed. "The net. Do you hear me, Ursus? We're riding into the net." Ursus continued his lethargic advance, raising his feet heavily as if they were caked with mud.

"Don't tell *me*," he seemed to say. "It was you who turned us around."

"But you know," said Arnth, "at least it's a silken net."

Here was the house at last, Tanaquil's house, with its orange tiled face and its saddle roof as red as Tanaquil's poppies. A redheaded house, thought Arnth with a surge of affection. *Like me, poor thing. But no freckles.*

It was afternoon. He had paused in the fields beyond the town to find food for himself and Ursus. At a prosperous farm house a kindly woman had fed both of them on grapes, mash, and cheese, and allowed Ursus to lick the pot of a Corn Sprite. Then they had driven to the foot of Sutrium and hailed the keeper of the drawbridge, the same ill-mannered chap who had searched Arnth's wagon on his recent departure. Admitted with the observation that bridges were not intended for heavy wagons and fat bears, they had clattered up the ramp and into the town.

Perhaps they would find Vegoia at Tanaquil's house. Spying out the place? or, Tinia forbid, playing her spells? Precisely the nature of her spells, Arnth could not predict. Sorceresses were highly versatile: they could read the future. They were rustic physicians, healing fever with gentian roots and headaches with willow bark; they manufactured potions for unrequited love and poison for disposing of a rival; and according to hearsay, they could change their shape at will and fly through the air or creep along the ground.

He thought it best to announce his coming. He had no wish to surprise anyone, certainly not Vegoia. He blew a cheerful blast on his flute. Ursus' walk became a gallop, and they rolled down the street as if they were hungry and the house was the world's largest honey cake. Soon, he felt like his music and the rush of his cart, swift, gay, and careless. He played of love opening like a morning glory, to shelter lovers in its blue, willowy walls. The music seemed spell and amulet. Nothing of evil could mar such an afternoon.

The gate flew open as if the garden had expelled its breath, and a hot and angry Vel exploded into the street. Oblivious to the wounded gate behind him, which hung like a broken wing on a single hinge, he sprang onto the cart, his toes scurrying up the side like fiddler crabs, and began to shout at Arnth:

"You were not supposed to weturn! You were not supposed to weturn!"

Arnth was dismayed by the boy's outburst. He dropped the reins and clapped Vel's shoulder. "But Vel, I thought you'd *like* to see me!"

Vel's anger evaporated and left him dour and subdued; somehow reduced in size. Arnth expected him to cry.

"Sweet musician," he wailed, "I told you not to weturn," and Arnth realized that Vel was not so much angry with him as afraid for him. Before he could ask the reason and learn the whereabouts of Vegoia, Tanaquil burst from the gate. Then, she was running beside the cart and crying, "Wait, Arnth, let me on," while Ursus was looking back with a crafty eye, as if he intended to stop so quickly that Tanaquil's momentum would carry her into his clutches. Arnth leaned from the cart and lifted her up beside him on the opposite side from Vel, who glared at her with the ferocity of an Ursus with two good eyes. She wore a tunic of saffron-colored linen imported from Lydia. Her dark hair had burst from its knot and spilled onto her shoulders, like black-skinned grapes clustering down a vine. Running had heightened the redness in her cheeks. For the first time, she did not look like the cultivated product of a town garden. She looked, thought Arnth, both flushed and delectable, a perfect dish for a hungry man's repast. Not his, however. Vegoia had totally spoiled him for lesser feasts. Who is content with chicken after pheasant?

"Arnth," she gasped. "You've come to help Vel, haven't you?"

They drove down a street where orange, red, and blue houses alternated with rocky, rose-tangled hillocks. It was as if the earth had grown the houses as well as the roses, and the men and women, fluttering in their robes from door to door, were hawk moths gathering pollen. People waved at the cart and its colorful occupants, and the ragged girl, the one whom Arnth had previously given a ride, hurried down the street to alert her friends that flutist and bear were back in town.

Briefly Arnth explained to Tanaquil about the arrival of Vegoia. Briefly Tanaquil replied that she had met Vegoia and heard about the evening on the lake.

"I expect she told you about the dinner she fixed," said Arnth lamely. "The pasta was delicious. A Corn Sprite gave her the recipe."

"She told me about dessert," said Tanaquil. "Never mind, you don't have to explain. I know all about young men and their needs. A good dinner and a saucy bedmate. Does that sum it up?"

Before he could argue with her addition, she changed the subject. "Tell me what Vegoia plans to do here in town."

Arnth, who was no more informed than Tanaquil, turned to Vel, who, between his glares at Tanaquil, was beaming at him with naked adoration as if to say: "Look at *me* riding beside my hero."

"Vel, tell me what is going to happen. How is Vegoia going to get you out of the town?"

"Through the gate."

"I didn't think you were going *over* the gate. I mean, how will you slip past the guards?"

Vel shook his head. "Who knows."

"Don't you?"

"Vegoia knows."

"Is she going to use her spells?"

"Who knows?"

"Where is Vegoia now?"

Vel evaded the question. "Leave the town, Arnth!"

"You're afraid someone will be hurt?"

Vel said nothing.

"But I can't leave town. Not without Tanaquil. You must promise me that no harm will come to her."

Vel said: "My friends will not be hurt."

Supper that night was ludicrous and foreboding. Tanaquil had asked that Arnth be allowed to dine with the family instead of the slaves. Lars was divided between the wish to please his daughter and the wish to observe the customary formalities of aristocrats with traveling players.

"Otherwise, he won't play for us," said Tanaquil. "Will you, Arnth?"

Arnth was ready to say yes, he would play anyway, at such times he always ate in the kitchen with the slaves, but Tanaquil proceeded:

"I told you, he won't play. You want another mime, don't you, Father? What about the escapades of Zeus? Europa and the bull, for instance? I'm sure Arnth knows a good one about *them*."

Arnth opened his mouth to say no, but he could sing a good one about Pasiphaë and *her* bull, but Tanaquil closed the discussion. "It's all settled then. He eats with us."

Vel, together with the acquisitive Athenian, served a platter of roebuck garnished with chestnuts, along with a deceptively bland-tasting wine which inspired Arnth not only to sing his song about Pasiphaë and the bull, but to improvise details which would have shocked a bawdy Gaul. As for Tanaquil, she carefully mixed her wine with three portions of water, but the mixture remained potent.

"I'm Pasiphaë," she said in the midst of the mime, adding thoughtfully, *"Enamored.* And Vel is the bull." The sprite was approaching the table with a tray of lemons imported from Africa. She rose to her feet and with perfect confidence, if slightly erratic movements, took his hand and led him around in a circle, using her free hand to seize a lemon and raise it to her lips.

"You are not very—*taurine,*" she said, releasing him at last, returning to her couch, and looking pleased with herself for producing such an epithet. Lars was also pleased. Throughout the mime, he had clapped loudly and quivered as if he would like to join the players, perhaps in the role of Minos, the cuckolded husband. But inebriation had prevented performance.

When Arnth had finished his song, he suffered a moment of troubling clarity: like a spectator at an Etruscan circus, he saw himself and Tanaquil playing the fool in a ring which was soon to resound with nameless perils—fire, gladiators, beasts—in a word, with Vegoia's spells. Tomorrow the nymph was certain to be discovered and expelled from the town, if not imprisoned, for breaking the inflexible law that Weir Ones were only tolerated on the Ninth Day. Tonight, then, she would have to act; perhaps already had acted to drug the wine.

He studied Vel for a clue to Vegoia's intentions. The boy, surly when Tanaquil had told him to play the bull, had now grown excessively gay. He flickered in and out of Arnth's dazed consciousness, a white, naked wraith from a Bacchic throng, refilling the krater of wine and the cups of the three drinkers. His arms seemed entangling grapevines; and his grinning face, its mouth parted to reveal a thin, pink tongue, had become the mask of a devouring sphinx. When the boy loomed toward him, Arnth threw up his arms to make a shield.

Vel caught his hand and steadied it around a replenished cup, which he pushed to Arnth's lips.

"Sweet musician," he said. "Dwink. It is good for your music."

Arnth did not drink. Angrily he struck at the persistent hand and overturned the cup against Vel's body. Wine enveloped the sprite like blood from a wound. Repentant and somewhat steadied, Arnth removed a hankerchief from a pouch in his tunic, a white linen square aswarm with blue seahorses. Against the boy's chest, he pressed the cloth to a wet, clinging flatness, through which his fingers felt for the beat of a heart.

"You have no heart," he said, not as an accusation but as an expression of sympathy. Tears welled in his eyes: for Vel, wine-stained as if with blood; for Vegoia, the little girl pretending to be a sorceress; and for all their beautiful, heartless, childless friends on the lake. "Vegoia told me but I wished to be sure." Somehow he felt to blame for the heartlessness of the sprites. "Does it hurt you, my friend, having no heart?"

Vel removed the handkerchief, crimson with wine, from Arnth's fingers and clutched it in his hand.

"Never mind," he said. "Never mind, sweet musician."

After supper, Lars retired to bed, attended by the Athenian; Vel remained in the kitchen; and Arnth and Tanaquil walked in the streets to clear their heads. They found the marketplace in silent pandemonium. The Weir Ones had left the town, tipsy, no doubt, and clutching their newly acquired treasures: bracelets to grace a horn, ribbons to bind a mane, and a few practical items like files and adzes and shoes with wooden soles. For nine days they would not return. The merchants had closed their stalls and retired to their houses on the perimeter of town. No one had bothered to clean the streets; there were wine cups—Athenian red and Etruscan black—in broken abundance. There were empty wine skins and fly-ridden, rotting figs; and gross evidence that the Weir Ones— the Centaurs at least—were no more fastidious in their toilet than the horses they resembled. Sutrium prided itself on cleanliness; tomorrow the marketplace would be scoured by slaves with enormous brooms and buckets who would wash the refuse into the drainage ditches which ran beside the streets and joined the intricate sewer under the town. But tonight, the refuse remained as a visible reminder of the Ninth Day, when the town and the forest met with mutual suspicion and parted with mutual relief.

"Even the serval cats have gone to bed," said Tanaquil. "Usually they forage around the fish stalls. It looks as if we have the streets to ourselves."

"It's just as well," said Arnth, "or we might step on them. I still feel a trifle light-headed. Where did your father get his wine?" His tunic, he noticed, was stained with red; the sash at his waist was threatening to slide over his hips; and one of his sandals, its strap broken, barely clung to his foot. *Dionysus,* he thought, *would take me for one of his Satyrs.*

"From the vineyards around Sutrium. It did taste potent, didn't it? Did I misbehave?" She still had about her the air of a Maenad. Whatever flowers had adorned her hair survived in a single petal—rose, not poppy—which bent precariously above her left ear.

"Not really," he said. "You couldn't misbehave. You're not the sort."

She looked injured rather than complimented, but managed to buoy a smile. "Well, *you* misbehaved. Honestly, Arnth, when you started singing about the bull—"

"I suspect" said Arnth, "that the wine was drugged. Or—bewitched."

"Vegoia?"

"Yes."

"But why? Nothing happened while we were drinking, did it? She didn't make off with Vel."

"Maybe it was supposed to knock us out, but it only made us foolish. Anyway, there may be an aftermath. I think it might be better if we didn't go back to your house."

"Where else can we go?"

"To an inn."

Tanaquil looked at him with surprise. "An inn?"

"Separate rooms, of course."

"You would have said *one* room if I had been Vegoia, wouldn't you?"

"I might," he admitted. "But then, you're not that sort, are you?"

"You keep saying that," she snapped. (He seemed to have an art for bringing out the worst in women.) "No, I suppose I'm not. Sometimes I wish I were, or that people at least thought so. And sometimes I wish I didn't have to be either *that* sort, or the other, but some of both, depending on how I felt and who I was with. I wish I made a man feel—*ungovernable*."

"How do you mean?" he asked nervously.

"The way you felt with Vegoia."

There seemed no end to what Vegoia had confessed in the temple. Talk about *men* who kissed and told!

"Seriously," he said, "we should go to an inn. Or better, I could take you out of town. To Viterbo or anywhere you like."

"Father would never forgive you. He would misunderstand your motives and have you hounded out of all the Etruscan cities, if not shut in a chest like a criminal and thrown in the sea. It isn't my virginity he's worried about, but how I lose it. A nobleman's son would be permissible.

"On the other hand, if we went back to the house, woke Father, and told him everything—how Vegoia is coming to make off with one of his slaves—he would quite likely call on the king for soldiers, and Vel and Vegoia would end up in irons. All we can do is to go back and say nothing. Whatever Vegoia does, I don't think she will hurt me. I liked her, you know. And I certainly don't think she will hurt you. Not after last night."

"Especially after last night," he muttered.

"Besides," said Tanaquil. "I want to know what happens to Vel."

"So do I. He needs his lake. Do you love him, Tanaquil?" Now that his own affairs were not in question, he felt like an older brother inviting a sister's confidence and ready to give advice.

"I don't think so." she said. "But he stirs me."

"I know what you mean. Sprites have a way about them."

"How do they do it, Arnth?"

"I think they take the town out of us. With a sprite, it's always as if we were naked in the sun, and no part of us were less than good and beautiful."

"Vel makes me feel naked all right, but then I want to go and put a robe on. I feel ashamed."

"You shouldn't. He's just a healthy boy looking at you with admiration. I've looked at many a girl that way. He ought to make you feel like *that* sort of woman."

"It isn't his lust I mind so much. It's between his lusts. He doesn't even seem to like me."

"Possibly," suggested Arnth, "he's the same as Ursus, my bear, who doesn't like women till he gets to know them." ("If then," he started to add.)

They found the house as silent as the streets. At the entrance the porter rose drowsily from his stool.

"What should I tell him about Vegoia?" whispered Tanaquil.

"Tell him nothing." said Arnth. "It won't matter anyway. If she wants to get in, no porter will stop her."

Handing Arnth a lamp, the porter opened the door. "The master is asleep," he said, a thin, stooped fellow with bony shoulder blades, and added reproachfully, "Everyone is asleep. Or ought to be."

They found that Tanaquil's room had been invaded by the moon. The four walls sparkled with wintry light, the squat-legged couch loured like a wolf in the snow. They kindled a lamp in the niche above the couch and added a roseate warmth to the moon's chilling frost. Then they examined the room for other, more tangible invaders.

Tanaquil smiled. "You see; there are no sorceresses except the Lady Moon. You may leave me without misgivings."

"By the way," he said, "where is Bast? I thought he slept in your room, on his own little couch."

"Sometimes," she said. "Other times he likes to roam. I try not to interfere with his peregrinations."

"Let him peregrinate, but I'm coming back."

He went to the room of the slaves and exchanged his tunic for a loincloth. The room resounded with snores, and he noticed Vel among the sleepers. He knelt beside him, remembering that other night when Vel had prepared a bed for his "sweet musician" with cushions from the triclinium. Here again was the bed, with the same pillows hiding the same hard straw. He took a pillow and pressed it against Vel's cheek; when the boy awoke he could slide it under his head.

Stepping nimbly among the recumbent bodies, he left the room and returned to Tanaquil. Though she lay on her couch with a coverlet over her feet, she had not extinguished the lamp, which shared its niche with a bronze figurine of Tages and a stone water clock imported from Athens.

"I'll sleep at the foot of your bed." he announced. "I'm a light sleeper, when I set my mind to it. If anyone opens the door or climbs in the window, Tinia help her!"

"Her? Him is more likely."

"Vel wouldn't hurt anyone with malice. At worst, he's a hot-tempered boy."

"Do you think Vegoia would?"

"I don't know," he confessed. "There are—angers—in her." It was strange how suspicion heightened his desire. Somehow, he feared and loved her at the same time, and loved her more because of his fear.

"You look uncomfortable." said Tanaquil, rising from bed to fetch him a cushion from a chest of olive wood. "Or perhaps you would rather—"

She meant, he supposed, to offer him half of her bed, but her look and voice were free of provocation, and her body, shapeless now in a woolen nightdress, epitomized sisterly innocence.

"No," he said. "The floor will make me a better watchman. I think, though, we should leave your lamp burning. After the moon sets, the Weir Ones will have an advantage. They can see in the dark."

"I always leave it burning. Otherwise, I have nightmares. I have them anyway, but I wake up and see the lamp and the image of Tages, and it's all right."

"Tonight it will be all right. Remember, I come from the country. I have even wrestled a wolf."

"You can't wrestle sorceries."

He started to say, "What about sorceresses?" but thought the remark indelicate in the circumstances. That was the trouble with women. Once you became involved with them, in his case *two* of them, you had to watch your tongue. They were always ready to jump down your throat. He said: "Tages guard your sleep."

Hardly had he closed his eyes when he felt the assaults of sleep, a quick stealing lethargy in his legs, a tiny prickling along his arms, like the feet of marching ants. He froze his eyes into a taut openness.

He heard the monotonous drip of the water clock. Athenian, like most of the best inventions. Better than the old sundial, which lost its usefulness at night or on cloudy days. He began to count the drips. One, two, three ... thirty-six ... sixty. ... No, that was dangerous. Counting would put him to sleep.

He tried to shake his head; to sit up; to kick his feet. Then he knew that he was paralyzed; drugged by the wine from supper. Immediate drunkenness had been the first and the least of its consequences. He tried to speak. "Tanaquil" poised on his tongue but refused to leave his lips. He could only move his eyes, which he fixed on the door to watch for Vegoia's coming.

Strangely, he wanted her to come, alone or with

Vel; kind or threatening. To come with quiet steps and whisper his name like an incantation—or a curse; to die into his arms—or bind him with painful thongs. Lover or victim, he waited.

The lamp pulsed and expired. The moon dwindled and drained the light from the room; the lucent snow melted into gray. The dark smothered him like an airless sheepskin, and the drip of the water clock seemed the slow, continual tap of advancing feet.

Till the feet advanced in truth.

The door whispered on its wooden hinges. He saw the eyes, luminous, yellowly slanting, in the almost-darkness, and knew the slap, slap, slap of the webbed feet before he saw the eyes.

Vel paused, wary in silence. Behind him a score of ovals repeated in miniature his own slanted eyes; hovered beyond the door while Vel advanced, listening, into the room and stopped without surprise above the prostrate Arnth.

"Sweet musician," Vel said, "I made a couch for you in the room with the slaves. It would have been better had you stayed with them. Still, you will not be harmed. I will see to that." He fell to his knees, gathering Arnth in his arms, and rose unbowed by the weight; and Arnth, though he could not move, could feel the thin, strong limbs which held him with loving tyranny.

"I will see to that," repeated Vel, and left the room with a glance at Tanaquil.

The corridor writhed with cats. In the darkness, Arnth could only guess their sleekness and gold. But he saw their following eyes, and heard the agile flutterings of their feet. One of them grew impatient; hissing, sprang from the ground and tore at his arm, which dangled helplessly above the floor. He could feel the clawing pain; the limp swinging of his struck limb. He tried to scream.

"Bast, get back!" cried Vel, and aimed a vicious kick at the head of the long neck. A snarl died in the animal's throat; cowed, he sought the anonymity of the pack.

At last they reached the atrium. Vel did not seem tired. He paused to wade in the pool, luxuriatingly, and then he deposited Arnth on the couch and knelt beside him with solemn tenderness.

"Has the cat hurt you, my fwiend? Ah, he has left a wound on your hand. Now we are bwothers."

The cats circled the couch, scratching the legs, pawing the air, staring up at Arnth. Was this not their promised victim, carried before them, tantalizingly, through the corridor? Years ago in the forest, Arnth and his friends, the traveling players, together with some small trained animals—a monkey named Liber, a dog, a parrot—had met a pack of wolves, large, gray fellows with eyes the color of water in a swamp. But the wagon in which they traveled, the one which Arnth now owned, was slow and cumbersome with its load of passengers. One of the players had suddenly snatched up the monkey, a genial fellow dressed in a hat and tunic, and thrown him to the wolves. The wagon had made its escape while the wolves quarreled for the small sacrifice and shreds of his tunic flew above the carnage. Now, it seemed to Arnth that the liberated cats surpassed the bloodlust and cruelty of the wolves. Sudden freedom was not enough for them; they wanted revenge for their long captivity.

But Vel did not allow them a sacrifice—not yet. He brandished the same mysterious stones which Vegoia had sent to him by way of Tanaquil. His lips moved soundlessly and the cats responded as if he had cracked a whip over their backs. They flowed from the couch, assuming a single shape beside the pool, like an octopus drawing in its tentacles, and slithered out of the room and into the corridor.

"For a moment I feared for you," said Vel. "Even with my stones. There is much anger in those—"

With the silence of a moonbeam, Vegoia entered the room; a whiteness beneath the open, starry roof.

Her voice was sharp and imperious: "Have you hurt him, Vel?"

"No, but he may hurt Tanaquil!" Arnth would have liked to shout. But his tongue was an icicle in his mouth.

Vel's answer was petulant. "He has not been harmed. I have shielded him from the cats."

"Where are the cats?"

"They have gone about their business."

She seemed to grow large with anger. The little girl had become the Lady Moon, implacable goddess of the night's black pits.

"I meant you to use them only against the guards—here and at the gate of the town. Have you turned them on the house?"

"The house?" he laughed. "The whole town! I have sent them to find their friends—and their masters."

"And Tanaquil?"

"Some I have sent by way of her room."

VII

SHE WATCHED HIM leave the room, his feet slapping the tiles heavily, heavily, because of Arnth in his arms. She watched a myriad eyes extinguish themselves in the darkness after him and reappear, after an endlessness of racking minutes, without him. Serval cats. That much she knew from the pad of the feet. Though their bodies were almost shapeless in the dark, she could guess the long legs, the yellow fur liberally dotted with black, the full, black-ringed tails.

They were led by Bast. She knew his eyes. She thought his name until it boomed in her brain: Bast, Bast, Bast.

They surrounded her couch like soldiers returning to familiar stations on a city wall. Of course! They had come to shield her on this night of strangeness and fear. Gentle Bast, born in Sutrium and unacquainted with his fierce African kinsmen, had brought his friends to form a ring of protection. Against evil. Against the return of Vel.

She was not surprised when he sprang onto the couch and placed an affectionate paw on her arm. Often he slept beside her. Often he laid his head against her cheek. *Dearest Bast, your fur is warmth on a cold night. Friendliness. Familiarity. But where is Arnth? Where is my father? They too need your protection.*

He prodded her with his paw. Then, foot over foot, he mounted her body and peered into her eyes. He was a heavy animal; it was hard to breathe with the weight of his pressing claws. She felt the heat of his breath and smelled an acrid, salty scent which she did not recognize. Not only his scent was different. He looked somehow— alien. Perhaps she had frightened him with her stillness. On other nights she had cradled him in her arms. He peered at her with nothing which she could read. Slowly, with deliberate grace, like a trained leopard in one of the great circuses at Tarquina, he raised his paw.

Then she recognized the smell on his fur. It was blood. The prodding paw, the slow advance, and now, the fixedly staring, almost hypnotic eyes, were gestures shrewdly calculated to tease and torture her. He did not intend to hurry his play. His eyes looked as cold as a topaz under the water. Perhaps they had always been cold. But now she was able to read them without the sentimentalizing haze of her affection, and she grasped the terrible truth that love can never be compelled, from man, from sprite, from beast; that one who loves, however she longs for requital, however long she waits, may receive in return the reverse of what she gives, the dark side of the moon.

His claw flicked the air, narrowly missing her eyes. She blinked; it was the one response of which she was capable. He was pleased; he had made her flinch. The smell of blood seemed a slime of decay oozing down her throat. His purr became a rumble, satisfied, expectant, and than a snarl vibrating through her body like the tremor before an earthquake.

He held his paw like a club. She could guess its power. A blow to her head would stun her; a blow to her throat would rupture the large vein of life-giving, life-sustaining blood which throbbed between the heart and the brain.

Snarls of impatience rose from the cats on the floor. She felt their bodies strike peremptorily against the legs of her couch. Bast stiffened; his friends had told him to hurry; his next blow must not be made in play.

She did not see the hand which delivered her from his weight. She felt his absence like the passing of a fierce pain, the removal of arrows imbedded in flesh. Inexorable arms enclosed her in a coolness of rivers, a freshness of rushes and cicely, and wafted her through the air as lightly as if she lay on a little skiff adrift in the wind.

Vegoia laid her on the tiles beside the couch in the atrium. Beloved couch, which held the shape of Arnth! There was light enough from the roof to recognize him, his loincloth and his shock of hair. Fearful couch, which held also the gloom of Vel! She would have known his eyes in total blackness.

Vegoia motioned to Vel. "Take the cats. I will follow you."

"What about Arnth?"

"I will tell him what to do. Hurry now. Meet me at the southern gate. And gather the cats from the streets and the houses."

Vel hesitated above the couch. "Sweet musician, good-bye. You know I wished you well. Always." He left the room, waving his stones and leading the cats.

"Listen to me, Arnth,"said Vegoia. "I will tell you exactly what has happened. The stones in by bulla and those I sent to Vel, are cat's-eyes. According to tradition as found in our *Book of the Lake*, they are the actual eyes of Egyptian cats, crystallized by necromancers in the time of the great pyramids. Before the Etruscans came to Italia, the Egyptians came in their little spineless boats to trade and colonize. They were poor traders and poor colonists. Frightened of forests and homesick for river and desert. They lingered only a year. But they left behind them these very stones, a gift for my people, who had sheltered them on the lake.

"I as sorceress have the stones in my keeping. When I hold them in my hand—so—they allow me certain powers, the greatest of which is the power to summon cats from a great distance, and speak to them, or rather, think to them. Warnings. Commands. Yes. No. Come. Beware. Tanaquil saw me with the cats in the marketplace. I promised them freedom in return for helping Vel. I told them to come here tonight and wait for Vel and me outside the house. In the dead of night, with the town exhausted after market day, it would not have been hard for us to reach the gate, and the small garrison in the watchtower—four or five men at most, all but one of them asleep—would have been no match for cats which can strike through windows with the speed of Tinia's lightning. We would not have needed to lower the bridge. The river is easily waded in the summer.

"Meanwhile, Vel was to drug you at supper. I had dipped the stones I sent him in a potion of henbane and bark, and he in turn dipped them in your wine and that of the slaves. I did not want you involved with his escape—you yourself, the slaves, Tanaquil, or her father. You might have been hurt by the cats. Or tomorrow, risked the wrath of a town which does not lightly release its slaves.

"How, you wonder, did Vel understand what I meant for him to do? By means of the stones. As soon as he held them in his hand, I could think to him as I had to the cats. In the old days, when the sprites were new to the lake, we thought instead of spoke—communicated without any need for words. But once we had learned the tongue called Latin from the Centaurs, the thought-power left us; ebbed like a stream in a hot summer's sun. But the stones restore it to me.

"After the market had closed, I hid in a stall of woolens until the town was asleep, and then I came to this house. As you know, I came too late. Already, Vel had aroused the cats against the town. I had meant him to use the stones only to drug the wine. Or, if I failed to reach him, to use the cats only for his escape. I did not foresee that he would use them against the Sutrii. But you must not think that he bewitched the cats. He simply encouraged them to do what was in their hearts—to kill and be free.

"Now, this is what you must do. When the drug wears off, as it will in a few hours, go with Tanaquil to your cart. It has not been harmed, nor Ursus. By morning, Vel and I will have led the cats from the town. But another danger remains. The slaves.

Most of them have not been harmed. It was not against them that Vel directed the cats. When they find that masters are dead, there is no anticipating what they will do. You yourself have nothing to fear. They have always loved you. But Tanaquil is an aristocrat. One of their masters. *Get her out of the town*. Head to the south for Veii. And believe me, I never wished to murder a town. Only to rescue Vel."

She knelt beside him, at once maternal and ardent, and cradled him in her arms. "It seems that our last time together, you must lie in my arms like sleeping Endymion. I was never meant to be the Lady Moon, content with sleep—or memories. But memories will have to serve us, will they not? Remember me, then, my red-haired rustic. But—" She paused, pressing a hand to her breast, as she had with Tanaquil in the temple. "Do not be sad for me."

Still on her knees, she turned from the couch and spoke to Tanaquil. "And you. Once I might have hated you. But now, I think, I could love you as a sister—and give you advice. Virginity is a rose without scent. It grows sweet only with the plucking."

Merciful sleep descended on Tanaquil, only to leave her wracked by merciless nightmares in which a pack of cats terrorized the house and buried her father under a sea of claws. Painfully, gratefully she struggled into the light and out of paralysis.

And who was the red-haired god who knelt beside her, straight from the sun-drenched fields of wheat and barley? Arnth, who else, massaging her wrists with his freckled hands. Strong, homely hands, familiar as ploughed earth or baked bread. The nearness of him suffused her with warmth. Vigor flowed from his body; from his blazing hair and cherished freckles. *I am the wheat,* she thought, *and he is the sun. I have fallen in love with him, and not as with Vel in lust.*

She lifted her arms and twined them, weakly but insistently, aroung his neck, For her, it was a bold and meaningful gesture, eloquent of her love. But he treated her hands as those of a grateful friend and not a would-be beloved. He pressed them with bluff, comradely zeal.

"Thank Tinia! I thought you would never wake! I was ready to carry you to the wagon. You heard Vegoia before you fell asleep? Then you know we must leave at once."

"Must we?" she said. "I mean, just at this moment?" She leaned against him rather more helplessly than her condition required. "Let me rest a moment, Arnth."

"Rest in the wagon."

"Oh, very well," she sighed. "But—where is my father?"

Arnth said nothing.

Shame clawed at her like a spitting cat. Her only thoughts had been of Arnth. "I must go to him at once!"

"No," he said sharply. "There is nothing you can do for him."

"I'm going anyway," she cried. "If he's dead, he has to be given a proper burial."

"There isn't time. the slaves—"

But already she was lurching uncertainly down the corridor on feet which seemed surprised to rediscover their purpose. Arnth caught at her shoulder. She shook off his hand and plunged through the open door into her father's room.

Lars Velcha lay on his side, his face to the wall. He seemed to be sleeping. She hurried around the couch.

"Father," she cried. His mouth and eyes were wrenched to the grimace of a comic mask. His face was as white as linen pounded in a mountain stream. Only his throat was red.

She was instantly sick on the blood-sodden couch. She had never felt close to her father. Compared to her mother and brother, he had always seemed a mortal misplaced among graceful gods, but she had loved him as a sometimes bibulous, sometimes pathetic being who needed her love with the quiet urgency of a man bereft of his wife. She thought: *I have to be sick until I have vomited all the blood from my body and become, like my father, as white as linen. I have to be sick in order to punish myself.*

Arnth returned her to life. His hand was as solid and reassuring as a ship's rudder. "Come, Tanaquil; the slaves are starting to wake."

"They will help us bury him then!"

"I'm afraid they have other intentions. I caught the one from Athens—Kimon, is he called?—looting the house. He was still groggy from last night's wine. I managed to brain him with a handy vase and take his dagger. It may prove useful before we get out of town. But when he wakes, and the others too, they won't be concerned with burying their dead master. They are free men now. Some may try to harm you."

"But they loved me. They called me Tanaquil of the poppies."

"They seemed to love you when it suited their

purpose. At the time, a few may have meant what they said. But sudden freedom is like unmixed wine. It muddles the senses and clouds the memory—even the memory of love."

"I don't believe you," she cried, but she believed him, and saw in the eye of her mind—the eye which had once seen gardens—the truth of the cats and the slaves, the truth of the liberation which follows slavery. Vel had unleashed the pack. Alone or in two's and three's, trusted more than the slaves, they had sought the master's bed. Perhaps he wakes and welcomes them: "Khonsu, Nekmet, Apis. Here, come into my arms or lie beside me under the coverlet. . . ."

It is morning. The slaves stir on their pallets, sigh, stretch, and resume the monotonous ritual of the day. Some to the kitchen to pound wheat and bake bread. Some to the garden, armed with hoes and pruning knives. Some to the master's room with water for his bath or myrrh to anoint his skin.

But the myrrh he needs is for his funeral shroud.

And the slaves are free. At least till the hated soldiers come from Veii (but who, surprised by freedom, thinks of soldiers?); free to rifle the houses and loot the stalls in the marketplace and steal the offerings left in the priestless temples. Free to complete what the cats have begun and drag the surviving masters out of their homes, those without cats, those who bar their doors before they sleep; wives and children.

"I don't believe you." she cried again, in one last protest against acceptance.

"You don't understand, do you, Tanaquil? How a slave could turn on his master? I've eaten and slept with slaves. I've sung their songs and listened to their stories. Believe me; I know how they feel—and hate."

Her voice was small. "And you hate us too?"

"No. But I would if you locked me in your fat, sleek houses, as you did Vel!"

She had never heard him speak with such bitterness. Merry Arnth, quick with a song or a smile! Perhaps he hoped to shock her into obedience. Nevertheless, his words had the ring of truth.

She could hear the bodies of slaves as they scraped to life in their crowded quarters. Groans, the babble of voices, those of the drunk returning to soberness. Harsh voices; murderous. She opened the coffer which stood in a niche above the couch, removed a coin, silver, stamped with the image of Vanth, and placed it on the tongue of her father.

"If I can't bury you, Father, at least I can give you the fare to pay Charon. The gray ferryman will not make you wait."

They found that the porter at the door had grumbled for the last time. He sat on his stool, leaning his bony shoulders against the wall as if with sleep. It must have been thus that the cats had found him, and left him but not in sleep.

They found the cart unharmed beside the street. Ursus sat on his haunches, pretending to be asleep but peering through a half-closed eye at an over-curious slave who seemed to have theft on his mind. Apparently Vegoia had led the bear from the stable to stand guard in his master's absence. When he saw Arnth, he reared on his hind legs and spread his massive paws. Supporting Tanaquil with one arm, Arnth used his other arm to hug that huge and irascible bulk, and the bear enclosed both of them in what Tanaquil feared would be a crippling embrace, at least for her. But Ursus for once was gentle. He left her gasping but without broken ribs, and she knew herself forgiven for being a woman and accepted at least as a friend.

The streets had the look of a Bacchanalia, but freedom, not wine, was the great intoxicant. There were neither garlands of hyacinths nor staffs entwined with ivy; there were neither flutes nor drums nor clashing cymbals; but the cry of the liberated was a thunder of song, and the whirl of bodies, a Bacchic dance. Everyone recognized Arnth. He had sung for them as readily as for their masters; he had taken their children for rides. They had no reason to harm him, though one old hag, with the skin of a raisin, shook her fist at Tanaquil.

"Pitch her down to us," she cried to Arnth. "What do you want with a baggage like that?"

As they neared the end of the houses adjoining the marketplace, an Etruscan gentleman, clad only in slippers, ran across their path and shrieked that his wife had been murdered: would they stop and help him bury her?

"No," cried Arnth, "but we'll give you a ride out of town!" He had started to pull on the reins when a passing slave, armed with a club, delivered a blow to the poor fellow's neck and went on his way as casually as if he had just defended himself from the bite of a dog.

Tanaquil gasped: "We must help the poor man."

"His neck is broken, I think. Besides, they would kill you if we stopped."

Well then, she thought. *Slaves can murder their lords in the light of day, and nothing of order or decency remains to stop them except in this wagon, and what can we do against a town in arms? The world is mad; the Etruscan power was to last a thousand years, but chaos has come before its time, and the gods have fled from their temples.*

Chaos indeed had come to the marketplace, in the shape of Weir Ones. Centaurs, Fauns and Panisci, though as yet no Water Sprites, had returned from the forest to steal what yesterday they had come to buy. The sleeping square had shuddered into life, but its life seemed that of a mortally wounded shark, thrashing destruction even as it died. Assaulted by hooves and paws, the closed stalls were bursting like rotten figs and spilling Milesian linens the color of strawberries and silks imported from the East and green as the fabled emeralds of Atlantis. A female Centaur draped a fine robe over her flanks and cocked her head to admire the fit, only to have it snatched from her back by a sly Paniscus, who frolicked down the road trailing the cloth, with the woman in close pursuit.

Two half-grown Fauns were dueling cumbrously with shields and battle axes. One of them stumbled and fell to the street under his shield, while the other tried to escape with both shields and both axes, but lost them to an acquisitive Centaur, who snatched up the Faun along with his booty. Across the market, Panisci were starting to climb the columns of the temple to Tages and throw down the terra cotta images to eager friends, who held out their paws hopefully but missed as many as they caught and twitched their tails in angry frustration. For the first time, there were no kittens on the stairs of the temple. They seemed to have followed their elders in the feline exodus.

Unlike the slaves, the Weir Ones did not hesitate to attack the cart.

"There she is," screamed a shrill female voice, and Tanaquil spied the same Faun woman who yesterday had sold her the wilted asphodels. "Stop the bitch; she's getting away!" A Centaur, waving a candelabrum as a weapon, one of its candles still miraculously burning, reared in their path so hugely that even Ursus panicked, rose on his hind legs, and received a cracking blow to his skull. The cart lurched to a stop. Swearing at the top of her capacious lungs, the Faun woman flung herself onto Tanaquil and began to tear at her hair.

Tanaquil caught the woman around the neck—Tages, how she smelled!—and dug her fingernails into the leathery skin, which popped like a hard crust of sun-baked mud. The woman was so surprised that she forgot to swear. She flung a hand to her neck and drew it away with a smear of green blood. Before she remembered the precariousness of her position, poised as she was on the side of the cart, Tanaquil aimed a kick at her hairy haunches. She fell to the cobblestones, swore at a male Faun when he carefully stepped around her but did not offer help, struggled to her hooves, and hobbled down the street with groans instead of oaths.

"Did you see, Arnth?" Tanaquil cried. "Did you see how I beat her off?"

But Arnth was engaged in a running battle with the same Centaur who had stunned Ursus. The bear by now, his thick skull protected by an inch of fur, had recovered his senses and begun to move. The Centaur was loping beside the cart and trying to catch Arnth's shoulder between the brutal charybdis of his paws. He had already managed to rake Arnth's skin with his teeth. Arnth meanwhile, all at the same time, was trying to hold the reins, keep his seat, and evade the centaur's jaws. From the look on his face, he had suffered a painful, even if superficial, wound. He looked as if the next jolt might topple him from his seat. Somehow, he managed to draw a dagger out of his tunic and thrust it between the threatening jaws. Though the Centaur's head was more human than equine, his jaws were as wide and strong as those of a stallion. Had they managed to close, Arnth would have lost his hand. As it was, the blade of the dagger, pointed to the sky, pierced the roof of the Centaur's mouth. Bucking with pain and spewing green blood on Tanaquil's nightdress, he wheeled from the cart and bellowed frantically for help. No one helped him; the others were too intent on pillaging.

The gate was open, swinging on bronze hinges; the guard lay sprawled in the road, his throat cut, his own spear lodged in his chest (Vel's work, thought Tanaquil when she saw the spear; it was not enough that the cats had cut his throat).

"And the bridge is down," cried Arnth. "And there—the road to Veii! There's no one to stop us now!"

Behind them the buildings of Sutrium crouched in their orange, intimate communion with the earth; without a sign of massacre or invasion; comfortable-seeming, as mushrooms without torn roots or broken polls. As yet, no towers had been broken by catapults; nor temples blackened by fire. As yet. But there, a thread in the cloudless sky like a vein in the blue translucency of a jellyfish. Was that not a wisp of smoke? And there, above the palace, a wavering lance of fire. . . .

"They're burning the city!" cried Tanaquil above the roll of the wheels.

"Probably someone knocked over a candelabrum or a fire box," said Arnth without surprise. "I don't think the whole city will burn. Just a building here and there."

"You don't care, do you, Arnth?"

"I care about the people"

"But not the houses and temples?"

"No," he admitted. "There are too many towns in the world, too—"

"Too many nets," she finished, but not with reproach. For Tanaquil, who had lost her father, her home, and her town, felt amply repaid by one traveling player, whose hair was friendly fire instead of destroying, and whose hands could build house enough, hut enough for all of her days.

"But it's been too easy," she said. "Our escape, I mean, The open gates, the lowered drawbridge—"

"It's only to be expected," said Arnth. "When Vel and Vegoia left the town, they had to leave everything open behind them. After all, they couldn't raise the drawbridge from the opposite end."

"Do you think they knew the Weir Ones would invade the town?"

"I'm sure they didn't."

"But why didn't the Weir Ones raise the bridge after they entered? Surely they know about the Etruscan garrison, just twenty miles away in Veii. When commerce stops from Sutrium, Veientine soldiers will come to investigate."

"I don't think the Weir Ones planned their invasion. They just stumbled into it."

But the Weir Ones were less improvident than Arnth had suspected. The plain, it appeared, held more than vineyards and olive groves. A gully, a hill, an old farmhouse, seemingly forsaken, thundered into life. Out of a gully, down the hill, around the farmhouse charged a small army of whooping Centaurs. How such large and blunderous beings had hidden themselves in anything smaller than a forest, it was hard to say. But here they were, athwart the road to Veii. Each of them carried a club of knotted wood and each of them bared his teeth—big, ragged teeth like those of a shark—in a grimace of leering bravado. It was sad to envision the fate of the local farmers.

"They're holding the road against the Veientines," gasped Arnth, jerking the reins to turn the cart. "We'll have to make for the forest."

"The forest? But that's their home!"

"Maybe they are all in Sutrium, or here on the road. Anyway, there is nowhere else to go. In the forest, Vegoia will help us if she can."

"If she will. . . ."

"Go under the canopy," said Arnth as they entered the doubtful refuge of the forest. "You'll be safer there. We may have some stones thrown at us."

But Tanaquil was feeling as bold as an Amazon. The Centaurs had not even given chase!

"I don't mind a few stones." she said.

"I do," said Arnth. "If they hurt my friend Tanaquil."

"Oh, very well," she said, concluding that his use of "friend" implied an intimacy beyond mere comradeship. Stooped at the back of the wagon, she peered through the curtains and watched the road they were traveling, with its border of seventy-foot hornbeams: their feminine smoothness of bark and their delicate, wiry twigs belied the hardness of the inner wood, which farmers cut to make yokes for oxen. But she had seen hornbeams all of her life, while the wagon was new to her and, being Arnth's home, infinitely intriguing.

The canvas walls were painted with frescoes like the rock walls of a tomb, and she knew from the subjects that Arnth himself had been the artist. There was Ursus, sniffing at the foot of a honey tree and looking, like most portraits, a little glamorized, a little less huge and fierce than his true craggy self. And Vegoia—when had he found the time to paint her?—rising from a lake with water-silvered shoulders. Naked as Vel she was, and two thirds of her out of the water! Tanaquil resisted the impulse to smudge the hussy with her fist. Then she felt ashamed. Vegoia had saved her life, and Tanaquil truly liked her, if it was possible to like a girl whom you earnestly hoped you had seen for the last time. *Well,* thought Tanaquil, *I will ask Arnth to paint my picture and, who knows, he may have to rub out Vegoia to make room for me.*

The wagon also contained a couch in a state of advanced dishevelment, though its wolfskin coverlet smelled as fresh as uncut hay, and she pressed it to her cheek lovingly and imagined herself beneath its folds with Arnth, the two of them snuggled together against the approach of night, cold, and cats. What had Vegoia said to her about virginity? A rose which grows sweet only with the plucking. It was high time for the gardener.

In spite of occasional jolts, she managed to smooth the coverlet and then to plump the pillows which were made of a coarse green cloth stuffed with escaping goosefeathers. Her aristocratic hands, she was finding, were not unsuited to menial tasks. They had beaten off enemies in the town, and now they were keeping house for her man. It pleased her to call him her man. There was something delectably barbarous about a woman having a man instead of a husband. Knowing Arnth's fear of marriage, she was more than content to be his woman instead of his wife.

She continued her explorations. A bear-shaped lamp with an upturned snout hung from the ceiling. Beside the couch stood a small wicker chair and a balsam chest with handles like seahorses, but Arnth's clothes, she found, were strewn on the rush-covered boards of the floor. They included: (1) three identical tunics of shaggy green linen; (2) a domed hat which had shrunk to the size of a honey cake; (3) a loincloth whose green polka dots had faded and stained the white background: (4) a pair of sandals with agate clasps and a broken strap. Strange, the untidiness of his things made her want to cry. She felt as if she had invaded his secret heart without his knowledge, to spy on his habits and affections. But having launched her invasion, she did not intend to retreat.

She lifted one of the tunics and held it against the light from the rear curtains. The cloth had frayed; the color faded. Work lay ahead of her, she saw; work for her man. She folded each of the tunics and placed them, together with the loincloth and the dwindled hat, in the bottom of the chest. The scent of Arnth, she noticed, lingered in his clothes.

Yes, every man had his particular scent, less overpowering than Vel's, as a rule but discernible and definitely agreeable to an interested woman. Her father had smelled like leather and olive-oiled bronze. Arnth's scent was cool and clean, a little of hay, a little of chestnuts lying among ilex leaves and wild thyme. Touching his clothes, catching the scent of them in her nostrils, was almost like embracing him. He had never really embraced her, she recalled. She had felt his brotherly pat, his comradely arm but not his *man's* embrace of the woman he desired.

Flying stones or not, she had to join him in the driver's seat. She thrust her head through the flap just as the wagon pitched to a halt and almost tumbled her over the back of Ursus.

Vegoia stood in their path, and behind her an army of cats, the color of brimstone. She might have been a young Circe, parading the victims of her sorceries.

Tanaquil seized Arnth's arm. "Keep going!" she cried. "They will tear us to pieces!" She had glimpsed the murderous Bast. The cats, however, were not her greatest fear.

But Arnth ignored her. With a wild, triumphant cry, he sprang from the cart—Zeus, how he covered the ground!—and Vegoia opened her arms to welcome him.

And Tanaquil thought: *It is not yet time for my picture to join the gallery.*

VIII

SHE LOOKED mercurial to him; cool and elusive like the liquid metal obtained from cinnabar; as if, at his touch, she would sink in the earth to rejoin her element. He felt the lithe solidity of her limbs, the coarse fabric of her wolfskin, but could not believe that she would linger, woman-like, in his arms. He, who had loved her lightly, did not deserve to hold her in thrall. But mercury became fire, and fire warmed him without burning, and Tanaquil, dreaming, sweet-voiced Tanaquil, was a dimly remembered ghost in the corner of his brain, like a moth in a cobweb.

"Dearest Arnth," cried Vegoia. "The Fauns have laid an ambush up the Road. They have already killed some soldiers from Viterbo—dragged them from their chariots. There is nothing I can do to stop them in their madness. There are more of them in the woods. But I know a secret path to the lake."

"And you came to warn me, Vegoia?"

"Why else? When I heard that the Centaurs were blocking the road to Veii, I knew you would have to drive this way. My dear, you are wounded!"

"It's nothing." He shrugged. "Now that you are here." He burned with the closeness of her. Centaurs? Fauns? What had such brutes to do with a forest becharmed by love, the ultimate talisman?

"Arnth, did you hear what I said about the ambush? You look benumbed!"

"Yes, I heard you. But what about Ursus?"

"Unharness him. Leave him in the forest. He will come to no harm."

Ursus was not difficult. He lifted a clumsy paw, as if to extend his blessing on their journey.

Arnth hugged him. "Old friend, we'll soon be together again." Then he reached a hand to Tanaquil. How pale she looked as he helped her to the ground! Frightened, no doubt, by the cats.

"It's all right," he comforted. "Vegoia will see to us now."

A few yards from the path, they found an oak tree, tall as a dozen ship masts end to end, with leaf-swollen heights and bark like the backs of gnarled wood spiders.

"You see," said Vegoia. "There are knobs for your hands and feet. I will lead. Then you, Tanaquil. Arnth will come last to keep you from falling. Can you manage, Tanaquil?"

"I was climbing trees before I was six," said Tanaquil sharply. Then, more softly, almost with fear: "Are the cats coming with us?"

"No. They will stay on the ground."

"And when we come down?"

"You have nothing to fear from them any more. They have what they want."

Tanaquil stared at Bast. "But—he killed my father. Doesn't he hate me too?"

"He hated bondage. Now he is free."

"They ought to be killed," she said bitterly. "All of them. Bast, at least."

Hearing his name, he pressed insinuatingly against her leg; craving attention from his old mistress. She shuddered and moved away from him.

They began their climb.

Tanaquil did not hesitate to grasp the rough knobs and draw herself up the trunk. The mountainous nightdress helped to protect her body from the bark, but her unprotected hands began to bleed. Arnth felt her blood on the knobs.

"Tanaquil, wait and let me make you a bandage out of my loincloth."

She shook her head and reached for another hold. "You haven't enough to spare. Besides, your wound is worse than mine, and I haven't heard you complain."

When they reached the lowest branches, climbing became less arduous. It was rather as if they had entered a green waterfall, whose flowing of leaves not only eased their climb, but hid them from the ground.

"They can't follow us," Vegoia reassured. "Even if they saw us climb the tree, the Centaurs are too big and the Fauns can't manage their hooves off the ground. And now—"

And now they approached the town in the top of the tree. A town of birds, thought Arnth, when he saw the circular structures suspended from the branches. They were not, however, nests—not even the big hanging nests of the oriole—but temple-shaped houses the size of pithoi or storage barrels, with columns running around them and a little platform surrounded by a railing like the gunwale of a boat. The walls seemed carved from amber, whose orange translucence ran to yellow and brown and, catching the sunlight, seemed to leap into flames. Figures moved in the heart of the fire, like crickets caught in a space between burning logs, and fluttered, singing, through doorways between the columns and noisily strewed the air. In the broken but brilliant light of the morning sun, they looked like giant sparks cast off by a blacksmith's forge.

"Mellona, the town of the Corn Sprites," Vegoia said proudly. "Have you ever seen such airy loveliness?"

"It is made of amber!" cried Arnth. "I didn't think there was that much amber in all the Great Green Sea!"

"Honey, not amber. They gather it from the farmers and then solidify it into building materials. It is said that a secretion from their own bodies completes the process. They can make it hard for buildings or pliant for bridges, or chip it into small pieces for pottery and tools."

"The houses look like the temple to Tages," observed Tanaquil, her spirits improved, if hardly amiable. "Round, with columns."

"Where do you think the Etruscans found the prototype for their round temples? As you know, most Etruscan buildings are squares or rectangles."

"And there," said Arnth. "Those images on the roof. They look like bees!"

"Exactly. That is not a house but the shrine to Mellonia, the goddess of bees and patron of the town. If you were smaller, you could enter the door and see the image of the goddess, conceived as a queen bee. She is sculptured in honey."

One of the Corn Sprites detached himself from the whirling sparks and lit in Vegoia's hand.

"You remember my friend, Arnza. You met him in my house on the lake. His name, by the way, means 'little Arnth.' "

Indeed, Arnth remembered the sprite. They had shared Vegoia's feast. Milky wings sprouted from his shoulders. His head, with the aureole of golden hair and its alabaster skin, was that of a dreaming boy, like one of those Yazatas or angels mentioned by Zoroaster, the Eastern philosopher who had recently died in Iran. But his orange, perfectly round eyes were mischievous more than angelic. Everyone knew of farmers who stinted their gifts of honey and found their figs without juice and their cows without milk (though no one knew how a sprite could milk a cow).

Arnth extended his hand and Arnza lit on his palm; then, bouncing into the air, he gave Arnth's nose a flick of his three-fingered fist.

"He is welcoming you to his town," said Vegoia.

"I was not sure," confessed Arnth. "What does he do when he's angry?"

"Spits. But have no fear. Once they like, they never change their minds. Even if you step on them."

"You can understand his speech?"

"I know his gestures. We have never felt a need for words, though of course the sprites have a language of their own. When they seem to be singing, they are really speaking."

"You have always been friends with them?"

"My people and I, yes. Not the other Weir Ones. The clumsy Centaurs spill their honey and the sly Fauns eat the honey and fill the pots with glue which they boil from the hooves of oxen. Only my people know the way I am going to show you. Actually, it is part of a network of roads built by the Corn Sprites. They use it when they do not wish to fly—when the air above the forest is turbulent with wind or dangerous with eagles. Their engineers are second to none."

The engineers, Arnth saw, had joined the trees by narrow, aerial roadways, perhaps an inch in width, which swayed on the wind like suspension bridges. For Vegoia, Arnth, and Tanaquil, the roads served as ropes which they used to balance themselves as they moved from tree to tree. Sometimes, they moved with their feet on the roads and their hands grappling the branches above their heads. Sometimes, in the spaces without branches, they clung to the roads, their feet swinging in air, and inched hand over straining hand, to the next tree. The roads proved sturdily built; they dipped and swayed but held to their moorings.

At other times the tree fugitives had to leave the roads and negotiate thick-set branches whose egresses and ingresses, scaled to the foot-tall dimensions of the sprites, tore at their clothes and left their exposed members smarting with pain. Tanaquil's nightdress had disintegrated to a wisp of cloth which clung tentatively to her body. Arnth's loincloth had been stained to the color of bark. Both of them gasped with the heavy exertion of their flight, and Arnth, who because of his travels was more inured to the forest, wondered how the town-bred Tanaquil kept from faltering. Whenever possible, on narrow limbs, in leafy thickets, he supported her with his arm. Only Vegoia, spruce in her wolfskin, remained as fresh and buoyant as an unpicked water lily.

Arnza, meanwhile, their self-appointed guide, piped encouragement and led them through moss and foliage and labyrinthine branches which made a night of the day. Once, he spotted a Faun watching them from the ground and hoping, no doubt, to see them fall, and plummeted angrily down to buzz in his big, furry ears. The Faun threw up his paws and took shelter beneath a blackberry bush.

Vegoia laughed. "You see what I meant about a sprite when he does not like you."

"Was he spitting in the Faun's ear?" asked Arnth.

"Yes. And his spit is pure formic acid. It has been known to cause deafness or put out an eye."

They came at last to the place where the trees met the lake, and stood, as if on the ramparts of a walled town, in the branches of the last tree.

"There," Vegoia said, pointing to the lake and the Town of Walking Towers. "We are safe at last. No one will touch us on the shores of the lake." She skittered down the trunk with the speed of a hungry squirrel. Arnth and Tanaquil followed her with anything but squirrel-like speed. Tanaquil's hands looked as if she had been fishing for oysters in a bed of coral, and Arnth's shoulder as if he had been bitten by a small but zealous shark. Arnza, having delivered them to the shore, spiraled over their heads and disappeared among the treetops.

Vegoia walked to the edge of the lake and called to her friends in the town. Hardly had she raised her voice when a score of joyful canoeists flashed their paddles and aimed for the bank. Nude in the sun and shining like molded mica, they improvised a song to greet the return of the wanderers:

> "Where the lake and forest meet,
> Garlands bring we here to greet
> One whose hair is robin-bright,
> One whose hair is woven night. . . ."

Vel was among the paddlers. He slithered out of the water, shaking himself like an otter, and ran to the tree. Quite oblivious to Tanaquil, he drew Arnth to his feet and urged him toward the water.

For a moment it seemed to Arnth that the Vel who had followed his music in the streets of Sutrium, the boyish, innocent Vel before the night of the cats, had exorcised the grinning murderer. Or perhaps there had been no murders, nor invasion of Weir Ones, but only phantoms conjured by Vegoia's magic.

Arnth said, almost doubtfully, as if he hoped for an outraged denial: "Tanaquil's father is dead because of you. Half of a town is dead."

"But not you," said Vel. "Not you. The cats obeyed me. I thought to them with the stones: 'You are not to harm my friend.' "

"And Tanaquil?"

"Oh, *her*. I thought them nothing about her. Why should I? I had been her slave. Come now; my canoe is waiting for you."

By now they had reached the water, but Arnth released himself from the boy's possessive grip.

"No, Vel. I am going to ride with my friends," he said, and giving a hand to Tanaquil, followed Vegoia into another and larger canoe. The paddler grinned at Vel. "You see," he seemed to say. "Thy chose *me*." He dipped his oar and the craft shot on its way.

Vel cried after them: "But Arnth, it was not you I hurt!"

Vegoia said quietly to Arnth: "You are right to break with him for Tanaquil's sake. He has terribly wronged her. But do not judge him. Do not blame him for your own mistake in thinking him human. He is neither more nor less than he has always been."

"But how could he love me and want to kill my friends?"

"He loves you for your music. A Water Sprite's ears are sensitive beyond belief. We can hear an ant crawling up a blade of grass. You ravished his senses with the sweetness of your songs. He also loved your beauty. He had never seen red hair. I think at first he mistook you for a god, and he never forgot his first wonder. Had you been old or ugly, your music would not have charmed him. As it was, you and the music seemed inseparable. He once said to me: "Arnth looks as if he had been played by a god on a flute." But his love was selfish. Like the other sprites, he has no heart. He saw you only for what you were to him. *His* friend, *his* musician. Thus, he resented your other friends and loyalties. He has even begrudged your closeness to me."

"I did love him, you know. When I met him in Sutrium, I saw him as myself as a young boy. Hating cages."

"He is not a boy. He is twenty-nine. But in ways he is less than a boy. A small child, quick to love—and quick to destroy. Affectionate—and cruel. How many children dream of killing their parents, guardians, keepers? Smallness and weakness prevent them until they have learned the order and orderliness of the adult world. But Vel had the strength and the means. And it was I who gave him the means. Perhaps I am also one of the children."

"No," he said. "You are wise beyond your years. You have helped me to understand him. In a way, I wronged him from the first. I closed my eyes to everything except what I could pity. And then, as you say, it made me angry when I saw the cruelty which I had overlooked. Well, I see it now, and now I no longer have to judge him. But we can never be friends again. Because of what he did to Tanaquil."

All this time, silent Tanaquil had watched the shore, where a lonely figure crouched beside his canoe. It was hard to say if she were forgiving him or fearing him.

They spent the night in Vegoia's house. Vegoia shared her hammock with Tanaquil, and Arnth, a little offended by such an unsatisfactory arrangement, occupied the floor. He was tired to the bone. His shoulder ached, his hands felt raw and inflamed, and his body throbbed to one long dull and enervating ache which only Vegoia could assuage, and not with potions and unguents. The sounds from the hammock—a heavy breath, a turning body—exacerbated his pain. When the last light had flickered from the last house, and the Town of Walking Towers had become a blackness indistinguishable from the black, star-stippled waters, he fell asleep and dreamed that a large crab, persistent with vise-like pincers, was harming his shoulder.

Then it was morning. Vegoia knelt beside him. "Tanaquil is still asleep," she whispered. "Would you like to swim with me?"

"Yes," he cried so enthusiastically that Vegoia pressed a finger to his lips.

"Shhh, you will wake her!"

He followed her down the ladder into the lake, and once they had left the shadow of the house, she entered his arms and kissed him with cool yet passionate lips which tasted of tart pomegranates.

"Tanaquil shall have my house," she said. "We shall build our own."

"Where?" It was all he could do to gasp the question. Her kiss had taken his breath.

"We shall build a floating house and live like halcyons on the breast of the lake."

"Hollow a log like Vel's?"

A wistfulness entered her voice. "That is too slow, my dear."

Advised, if not materially assisted, by the Water Sprites, they built a raft of thongs and linden boughs with a central pole like a mast.

"But what about our *house*?" Arnth asked. "This is only a raft."

"Be patient," she smiled. "Our house is in the making. No, it is made!"

She pointed to the sky. An amber cloud, sustained by a host of Corn Sprites, Arnza among them, was settling toward the raft like a swarm of bees.

"A tent!" cried Arnth as the cloud enveloped the raft and settled over the pole which was not, after all, a mast.

"And woven of honey. The sweetness is still in the cloth."

"It is like the mantle of a Lydian queen!"

"But thinner and finer. And see! They have hung a pennant from the tip of the pole. An image of their goddess to watch over us."

"But how did you call to them? We've been together all morning."

"Remember that I am a sorceress. Perhaps I whistled to them when you turned your back. There are whistles inaudible to human ears."

"Whistle for Ursus then. He would like to see our tent."

"You mean, you would like him to *share* our tent."

"Yes," he admitted. "I worry about him in the woods. I would make him wash, of course."

"He is safe enough. The Fauns and Centaurs have no quarrel with bears. Besides, he has found a mate. The Corn Sprites told me."

"Ursus with a mate? He is too old!"

"Bears are never too old."

"But he doesn't like females!"

"I never said that he *liked* her. Come now—"

Together they entered the tent. They had woven a hammock of bark, grass, and fibers like the nest of an oriole, and now they covered the floor with rushes, whose flat, grassy leaves and greenish flowers, yellowed by sunlight strained through the walls, resembled a meadow on a sunny day. There were also chairs and an oven, earth-colored, rather like rocks or tree stumps in the meadow. There was no chest for clothes, since Arnth had discarded the remnants of his loincloth and Vegoia had given her wolfskin to Tanaquil.

Returning to the open deck, they thrust their long, oak-bladed paddles into the lake and guided their raft away from the shore and the well-intentioned but over-curious Water Sprites. In the middle of the lake, a strange windless calm, like the eye of a storm, enfolded them in a hush of peace.

Vegoia was infinite in love. Now she was young, virginal, wondering, as she numbered the marvels of his body—the big hands, clumsy and tender at once; the adamantine chest, redly dusted with hair; the hard thighs which tapered to powerful legs and ended, incongruously, in feet so small and narrow that they might have belonged to a girl. Her hands, like butterflies, fluttered over his body, shyly, modestly, as if his strength might startle them into flight.

Now she was wise and knowledgeable, mature in years and practiced in artifice: queen and temptress, Circe, Medea, Helen, playing his body like an Aeolian lyre and plucking a sinewy music from his limbs.

But he; he had no artifice with which to equal her. Tenderness paralyzed him. The touch of his hands, he felt, his rough farmer's hands, must bruise her skin or break her fragile bones. Once, he had loved her lightly and not lacked confidence. Now, he feared that the hot Vesuvius of his love must burn her to cinders and ashes.

"Dearest Arnth," she whispered. "I am neither Phoenician glass nor Athenian pottery. You would be surprised how much it takes to break me."

He loved her then with all the golden savagery of his youth, and yet with the gentleness of years; leopard and deer inextricable in his kisses, he raged without rending. Words were weak; pallid symbols of the heart's high urgencies. But his body spoke with wordless eloquence; with shouts or whispers, tumult or tenderness.

The morning was windless and calm. They seemed to lie in the heart of a copper shield laid down by a Titan, weary of battle.

Vegoia trailed her hand in the water. "You are hungry," she smiled. "You are watching my hand as if it were a fish."

"Yes," he admitted. "I was planning to make a hook and—"

"Hook? Not while I have my hands." She dove in the water, melting, it seemed, into the burnished copper, and returned to the raft with a large pike in her hands. Without the least squeamishness she removed the head with a small hatchet, primitive but newly sharpened, and wrapped the body in lily pads to cook in the oven.

"But we have no wine," he said. "You left your skins with Tanaquil."

"Will you never learn to trust me, Arnth? It is written in *The Book of the Lake* that love is the greatest inebriant, but man must have drink as well. Be patient. The fish is not yet done."

When the fish was done, the drink was at hand, ferried by Arnza and his friends in cups the size of a snail; a blend of honey and fermented blackberry juice. Arnth and Vegoia sat on the edge of the raft, eating the fish with their fingers and sipping the wine. Arnza, who chose Arnth's knee for his seat, joined them in a libation to the bee goddess while his friends returned to shore. Together they spilled some drops in the lake and Vegoia intoned a prayer:

> "Mellonia, queen of the bees,
>   Watch over the hive, our house;
>   We thank thee for the honey of our roof
>   And the honey of our wine;
>   May hours like petals enfold our honeyed love."

Arnza did not linger beyond the last of the wine. With his three-toed feet, he thrust himself in the air and, pausing to top Arnth's nose, followed the other sprites to shore.

"He is very respectful of love," said Vegoia. "Ordinarily, he would spend the day with me, but today he did not wish to keep us from our pleasure."

"Perhaps he has gone to see Tanaquil," said Arnth. He had hardly thought of her for a whole day! It was he and not Arnza who ought to pay her a visit. "We must go to see her ourselves. She is sure to be lonely."

"Today?" said Vegoia without enthusiasm.

"Tomorrow."

Imperceptibly the flaxen morning blazed into afternoon, which trailed into dusk like a great queen with saffron robes. But the night was sad for Arnth because of Vegoia. She served him cheese and bread and small red apples the size of plums, but spoke little and ate nothing.

"Vegoia," he asked, "why are you sad tonight?"

"Summer is followed by autumn. Day by night. Today we were very happy."

"But the gods brought us late to love. Surely they owe us more than a day!"

She sat up sharply and pressed a hand to his mouth. "Hush, Turan will hear you. Or one of the darker gods. Never tell them how much they owe. That is for them to say, not us." She took his hand. "Perhaps it is the weight of my love which makes me sad."

"To me," he said, "love is a weightlessness—I

feel like a thistledown over an olive grove. And a sweetness—I feel like a Corn Sprite filling his cheeks with honey."

"Weight, weightlessness, sweetness, whatever we call it, there can be too much. A surfeit. I think that tonight you should go to Tanaquil. She also loves you, my dear."

"Tanaquil? Don't be ridiculous! If anyone, she still loves Vel, in spite of everything. Certainly not me."

"She never loved Vel. She merely desired him because he was the first to break her dream. You, she loves. And why not? I do, and I am harder to please."

"We'll both go. We'll take her some blackberry wine."

"It is you she wants, and not as a friend. Go to her, Arnth."

He looked at her with dismay. He had almost forgotten the fickleness of her people. "But it's you I love!"

Her laugh was forced and harsh. Such laughter rang from the brothels of Corinth and Sybaris. "This has nothing to do with love. You will simply be easing her loneliness." Turning her back, she walked to the hammock and slumped into its folds.

He did not dare to touch her, so remote she had grown, and still. Like a pearl in an oyster, he thought. He remembered that, after all, her feet were webbed and her temples sprouted fins. Alien, that was the word. Very well, he would go to Tanaquil and find more welcome than in his own tent!

But Tanaquil was not yet used to the freedom of the lake. He would have to lessen his nudity. With the help of Vegoia's hatchet, he cut a loincloth out of a lily pad—he simply cut holes for his legs and drew the pad up around his waist and fastened it with a strip which he tore from the bottom of the tent. Not until he entered Vegoia's canoe, moored to the raft, did he notice the hatchet which, unthinkingly, he had kept in his hand like a weapon. A weapon? Nonsense! A useful tool. Vegoia had demonstrated its usefulness when she beheaded the fish, and he, when he made his loincloth. He would take it with him as a gift for Tanaquil.

IX

SHE WAS THINKING about him when his dear, infuriating head appeared at the top of the ladder; thinking of Water Sprites, Corn Sprites, Vegoia, Vel, and life on the lake, but forcing her thoughts to revolve around Arnth without alighting, like bees with a cluster of grapes.

But here he was, and in time to share her dessert of blueberry cakes (a trifle brown, perhaps, a trifle hard, but after all, she was new at the oven).

"I brought you a hatchet," he said. "For cleaning fish."

Honestly, she thought, *what does he take me for, a fishwife?* But she forced a smile and accepted the hatchet as if it were a gift of flowers. Then she offered him a blueberry cake.

"You see, I'm learning to cook. Do you think I'm making progress?"

He accepted the cake with zeal and began to eat, but ate less rapidly after the first bite and grimaced as if he were chewing rocks. Perhaps he had poor teeth.

"Do you think I'm making progress?" she repeated.

"Ursus would approve," he smiled wanly.

No doubt, she thought. But Ursus also approved of stale fish and beehives. Never mind. She would take the remark as a compliment.

"I think your loincloth is charmingly rustic," she said. "Green is your best color. We're both making progress, aren't we? How do you like my wolfskin? One of the sprites gave it to me. Of course I had to make alterations."

"I thought Vegoia gave you hers."

"It didn't fit," she snapped, though the one she was wearing appeared to have come from a remarkably fat and bedraggled wolf. "We'll be true woodsmen before long," she continued, ashamed of her pique. "Sutrium, by the way, is still in the hands of the slaves and Weir Ones. They're working together, and only this afternoon, I understand, they beat off some soldiers from Veii. One of the Lake Dwellers saw the whole thing. But I wouldn't want to go back even if the city should fall. Would you?"

"No. I like the lake too much."

"Of course you do," she said, the edge returning to her voice. "You and Vegoia."

He looked embarrassed and guilty. Silence blew like a wind between them, extinguishing the candles of their conversation.

She forced herself to speak of trifles. "You see," she said, pointing to a bowl of chestnuts. "I've become a woodsman in more ways than one. I picked those in the forest today."

"You go in the forest alone?" he cried.

"Oh, no, always with the sprites. They are very

kind. Sometimes with Arnza too." His concern pleased her. Perhaps she ought to have emphasized the dangers.

Again, the winds of silence, the sputtering candles.

"Take a chair," she said at last. "Here, we can sit by the Port and watch the water. You have no idea the things you can see. This morning I saw a large water rat towing a garland of lilies. He would tow a bit, climb on the garland to rest, jump in the water and tow again."

"I like your hair," he said. "You don't capture it any more with a fillet. It escapes over your shoulders."

"I haven't any flowers in it."

"You don't need any. It is flowered with light from the lamp."

"You were sweet to visit me, Arnth. I've missed you."

"Vegoia and I wish you would visit *us*. Any time you like."

"I might come at the wrong time."

"There is no wrong time for you." He took her hand.

She made a slight pretense of retrieving her hand. Then, as if it were a woodmouse settling into a nest, she let it relax and warm itself in Arnth's big fist.

"What would Vegoia say if she knew you were here with me?"

"Why, nothing," he said, surprised. "Vegoia sent me."

She shot out of her chair like a stone from a slingshot and Arnth threw up his hands as if she had threatened him with blows. Well, she should have! Charun take his honesty! Would he never learn the niceties, the gracious evasions, which women like in a man?

"You can tell Vegoia that I don't want her leavings! I can find a man of my own. I've had three invitations today from the sprites!" (Actually, it was two, but a little exaggeration would enforce her point.)

"I enjoyed the blueberry cakes," he stammered and, getting a growl in response, climbed down the ladder and into his canoe, while Tanaquil, resisting the temptation to drop some cakes on his head, busied herself with the remnants of supper and energetically ignored his retreat.

"Uncouth farmer," she muttered, and ran to the window to watch his departure.

Once he had left the area of the town, he raised his paddle and looked over his shoulder at her house. Ducking out of the window before she was seen, she fell to the floor and started to number his faults: hands too big for his height; freckles beyond counting; honesty which bordered on rudeness; a stout resistance to domesticity. . . .

It was then that she heard the canoe in the Port. She jumped to her feet. *He has come back,* she thought, *and this time Vegoia has not sent him! Restrain yourself, Tanaquil. You can't run to the ladder and fling your arms around him as he steps into the room. You are no longer a child, but a woman of years and experience. Sophistication must be your guide and weapon. Ask yourself: What would Vegoia do?*

Vegoia would busy herself with domestic tasks and then, when he entered the room, turn to him and say, quite casually and as if she were expecting any number of men: "Oh it is you, is it?"

She turned and said, quite casually. "Oh, it is you—"

It was not. It was Vel.

He looked as blue and dazed as a hunter lost in the snow. His eyes were wet and swollen. The fins at his temples were frozen to the hardness of knives.

She did not know if she should fear or pity him. How had she ever desired him, this blue, inhuman, unknowable animal who came toward her without words and without sound except for the slap, slap, slap of his webbed toes?

"Vel, what is it? What do you want?" She felt for the hatchet on the table—a crude, small tool, but also a weapon. Her fingers closed on the wooden handle.

"You made my fwiend hate me. You took his music from me."

"He doesn't hate you. He's hurt, that's all. Because of my father."

He had stopped at last; he seemed to study her. She raised the hatchet to show that she was armed.

"He played for me," he said. "When I followed his chawiot, he called me fwiend. But you—you wanted him for yourself. You told him lies about me."

"Vel, I never told him—"

He sprang like a serval cat. She threw up her hands as a shield. She did not strike him with the hatchet. It was he who struck the blade and simultaneously bore her to the floor, his fingers sharp at her throat. The voluminous wolfskin softened her fall. Nevertheless, she gasped with the weight of his body. Then, his fingers fell from her throat and the weight grew inert.

She rolled him onto his back and knelt beside him. He stared beyond her, bemused and very quiet. He seemed to be sleeping with open eyes; perhaps he was lying on his hollowed log and dreaming of garlands woven from water lilies, or phoenix-colored flamingoes, fiery atop their nests. The blade of the hatchet had cloven his skull; blood oozed from the meeting of skin and stone. His body seemed diminished. How slender he was, and young, with his thin, pinched shoulders! Not killer nor beast, but a vulnerable, dying boy.

"I never meant to hurt you," she said. "From the very first, I only wished you well. And yet I brought you to this."

"It was the gods who brought him to this."

She had not heard him climb the ladder. Though his arms were a little room of warmth and refuge, she thought. *It is the old dream, and the arms will fade to the insubstantiality of mist, of smoke, of dust.*

But freckles were much too real for a dream. They burned with the bright immediacy of Arnth, the farmer, the piper, the driver of big-wheeled wagons drawn by petulant bears.

"I looked back at your house," he said. "I saw Vel's canoe and came after him. I was afraid for you."

It was then that Vel spoke. His voice was distant and thin. He seemed to be speaking from the bottom of a deep well. "Have you forgiven me, fwiend?"

"Yes, Vel. Yes!"

"Sing for me, sweet musician."

"What about, Vel?"

"Fwiendship. Death."

Arnth sang about gods and heroes: Achilles

grieving for the death of Patroclus; Hercules weeping for the lost Hylas. But friendship, he seemed to say, survives the grave. Achilles, draw your bow, Hercules wield your club, and rout the demons who haunt the banks of the Styx! Friendship awaits you on the far shore. In the meadowlands of Elysium, Patroclus is resurrected, Hylas is found.

She closed her eyes. She felt the thunder of wings (or was it the beating of her own heart?), and saw through her clenched lids a white radiance (or was it the fitful flaring of a lamp?), and fell to her knees before the coming of Vanth, the kind, the implacable. . . .

His freckled cheeks were cobwebbed with tears. She had never seen the tears of a man. She could only brush his cheeks with shy fingertips.

"Please don't weep," she said. "You'll wash away your freckles."

He took her hand. "Vel tried to hurt you, didn't he?"

"Yes. But I never meant—this."

"He would have killed you, I think. There was great violence in him. Now we must tell Vegoia."

Vegoia led the procession through the forest. She wore a tunic of leaves, miraculously joined by threads from a spider's web, and somehow she moved with the hush, the fixed eternal-seeming of a natural object, a stone, a root, a hill. Arnth walked at her side, piping the errant Vel to the portals of death with the sound which in life had been more than life to him. Behind the nymph and piper walked the sprites, bearing the wooden sarcophagus which held their friend and the objects which he would need for his perilous journey through the nether lands: a knife to battle the demon, Tuchulcha; a bow and arrow for hunting; and a bulla with strong-smelling asofoetida to repel the griffins and demons along the Styx.

Tanaquil walked in the rear of the procession, a solitary figure whom no one blamed but who could not bring herself to walk beside the boy she had killed; and last of all came the cats from Sutrium, an endless yellow river flowing as if with a single current and to a single sea. Vel had freed them; Vel was dead. They had come to mourn him.

The mourners left the trees and began to climb a hill which seemed an unbroken thicket of blackberry brambles. A narrow path crept wispily up the slope and spared their legs the tiny hooked thorns. Close to the top, Vegoia halted and turned to Arnth.

"It is not permitted that you should see the Mundus. You were Vel's friend. But not of his race. You and Tanaquil must return to the lake. The cats will protect you in the woods."

Side by side in the path and stemming the yellow flow of cats, Arnth and Tanaquil watched the Water Sprites as they climbed the hill and slid, like the tail of a dragon, over the bristling crest.

"Are they going to burn his body?" asked Tanaquil.

"No. Fire is the enemy of water. Vel disliked fire. Vegoia told me that they will leave his sarcophagus on a ledge in the mouth of the Mundus. Tonight, when even the owls are asleep, his soul will emerge from his mouth and sink down the walls of the pit and into the earth and so to the river where Charun waits with his ferry."

"There will be demons along the way?"

"Yes. But Vel has weapons and charms to protect him. And Vanth will be his guide. Once she has claimed a man, she becomes his friend."

"And across the Styx. There will be music?"

"Music always."

For Tanaquil, the days which followed the burial were indistinct and indistinguishable, a grayness in spite of the sun. She grieved, but did not know the object of her grief, whether her father or Vel or perhaps herself, unloved in love; or every man, caught in the labyrinth which the gods called life and bestowed as if it were a gift. *We whirl and claw,* she thought. *Rend each other in fear, doubt, and anger. But where is the final turning of the maze? Where is the Ariadne whose scarlet thread will lead us to the light?*

Arnth and Vegoia treated her with a grave courtesy and a deep, unspoken affection. Complete in themselves, they pitied her incompleteness. Every morning they paddled to visit her and took her in their canoe around the lake and explored inlets roofed with grapevines or dug along the banks for the stone ax blades of the old Terremare people. Vegoia taught her to fish with her hands and where to find honey trees, blueberry bushes, and edible mushrooms.

"Even the deadly mushrooms have their use," she explained. "You can tip a spear with the poison. The Fauns and the Centaurs are still holding Sutrium, but once they return to the woods, they will not look kindly on you and Arnth. It is wise to carry a spear."

But Arnth and Vegoia, she learned, were not

after all the fortunate lovers in a forest idyll. Vegoia was plainly ill. The eternal girl, nymph of the waters, had become a woman with pain-haunted eyes and the pallor of January. Her beauty was undiminished, but she was beautiful in the way of frost on the bronze-green leaves of a cypress tree, or an albatross on a sunless afternoon, suspended between the clouds and a tarpon-colored sea.

But Vegoia refused to admit her illness to Arnth and Tanaquil.

"Water Sprites never get sick," she laughed. "We drown, we are killed by lightning or wild animals. Or we get old and go to the Mundus. But sickness? Turan herself might envy our health! It is grief which makes me pale. Grief for Vel. He was very dear to me, you know."

As for Arnth, he rarely left her side, but he hid his solicitude behind a mask of gallantry. He looked as young as when he had come to Sutrium. He was still the rustic god, abundant with freckles and quick to laugh. But such a sweetness had exalted his face so that Tanaquil sometimes caught herself staring at him with a wonder akin to worship. Thus, ironically, she loved him most in his love for Vegoia.

One morning Vegoia paid her a visit with Arnth. Tanaquil offered her a cup of wine and honey, and when they had spilled libations to Mellonia and the gods of the earth, Vegoia spoke.

"Tanaquil, as you know, there are two kinds of wanderers. The first kind wanders because he must. He follows a will-o-the-wisp which he never expects to catch. How many miles to the highest cloud? Where does the phoenix build its nest? These are the questions which he asks himself.

"The second kind wanders only because he has

found no reason not to wander. Give him a reason—a house, a wife, a friend—and soon he forgets about the other side of the river and the dark side of the moon."

It was often Vegoia's way to approach a subject by indirection. Tanaquil's way was more direct.

"Which kind is Arnth?"

"The second kind. He is happy, I think, on the lake. He has even found Ursus. Every afternoon they fish together in the shallows, and neither one of them looks as if he wants to hit the road."

"Certainly not Arnth," said Tanaquil. "Not while he has you."

"But if he should lose me, Tanaquil, he would wander again, would he not? Unless he should find a second reason to linger. Do you know of such a reason? Of one who will never fret when he wants to fish with Ursus, and never chide him when he eats twelve honey cakes in six bites and asks for twenty? One who will love him all the more for his red hair and freckles, his big hands and little feet? Do you know of such a one, my dear?"

"You know I do, Vegoia. But he still has you, hasn't he?"

"Perhaps I shall leave him," she said with brittle levity. "I am a lake dweller, after all. Fickle. Prone to wandering myself. And, of course, heartless."

X

"It is my secret place," Vegoia said. "The Corn Sprites showed it to me, and I used to come here alone when I was very sad or joyful."

"There was no one you wanted to bring with you?"

"Not then. You see, it is a place for love, and sacred to Turan. She brought Adonis here, and mourned him here, after the boar had killed him."

Leathery grapevines, anchored to red-barked dogwood trees, netted a windless bower whose floor was moss; and thickets of sweetbriar sprawled in the sunny spaces beyond the vines, their dark green leaves exhaling a myrrh-like fragrance denied to their pink, clustered flowers. In just such places the Fauns and the Centaurs danced their midnight orgies and howled at the moon. But not here; not in this secret place, where Turan and not the Moon was queen; Turan, who scorned their lustful ways, their ignorance of love.

"You see, the sprites have proceeded us. They have hung the branches with images of the Goddess."

"But the images look like birds!"

"It is thus that they see her, a scarlet bird. When the wind blows, the feathered images sway and emit sweet pipings from the intricate works in their breasts."

"But we have no gifts for the goddess."

"We have the rarest of gifts." She drew him beside her onto the moss. "Ourselves. Libations and hecatombs are all very well for the other gods. But Turan is a woman. Burnt offerings offend her delicate nostrils. But the sight of love is incense and wine to her."

He smiled. "How do you know her so well? Till a little while ago, you weren't among her worshipers."

"But I have always known her ways. I was simply waiting until I could worship her in the right way."

"What about me? Do you think I will please the goddess?"

She shook his hand and studied the palm as if she were reading his fate in the branching, furrowed lines.

"Yes, she would like your hands. Strong yet kind. And your hair would please her too. It is like the fire from one of her altars."

"But my freckles. What would she say about those?"

"Human. Endearing. She wearies of perfect beauty. Maris, lordly as bronze. Adonis, unflawed marble. Perfection is easier worshiped than loved, and Turan wants most of all to love. In fact, I had better stop numbering your graces, or she will envy me!"

"Then I shall number yours. But where shall I start? There are so many of them!"

"Hush," she said. "Hush, my dear, and love me," and stabbed him to knowledge of her fragile mortality. "I am neither Phoenician glass nor Athenian pottery," she had said, but he felt that the touch of his fingers might shatter her into a thousand fragments, a thousand iridescences lost in the hands of the rainbow or the sky various with stars. Felt as if words and imperfect gropings of flesh no longer possessed her; as if he could speak and touch, and yet the essential part of her would slip irretrievably beyond his grasp; burst and dissolve on the air like a vial of sandarac.

"You're going away from me," he said.

She pressed an icy hand against his cheek. "Listen to me, Arnth. Listen to poor thin words and understand them as if they were luminous. You know how the hunters build a fire in the woods on a winter day. Their hands are numb with holding their bows and nets; they envy the beasts their deep-dug nests. Then, the fire leaps up like the walls of a Corn Sprite's house—yellow and red and orange, and most of all amber. And smoke, not coarse and black, but blue and dusky against the winter sky. Amber fire and blue smoke. And the hunters are warmed. Richly. Not only their bodies. Shall they reproach the fire when it dies to embers? Or the smoke, when it thins and fades above the sere trees? A woodfire was never meant to be enduring.

"There is a second kind of fire. A hearthfire, which burns with a low, pale flame and little smoke, but burns all winter, fed each day and tended by careful hands. In the best of worlds, woodfires and hearthfires would make a single flame of rich colors burning always. Perhaps the best of worlds is the Elysium which lies beyond the demon-haunted cliffs and the dark Styx. Perhaps. But here, it is not so. And it is the measure of a man that he can move from woodfire to hearthfire without bitterness, without reproaching the gods, his enemies, or himself. Let him remember, if he will, the blue and the amber, but not with regrets for what he has lost; rather, with gratitude for what he has found: a brief, bright burning in a wintry forest."

He took her in his arms. "Why do you speak in riddles? Woodfires. Hearthfires. I am your fire, Vegoia! Warm yourself in my arms!"

"Forgive me if I have puzzled you. I am only saying that the human heart—from what I have seen of hearts—was not intended to poise always in the flush or worship, like a devotee standing in front of a temple. There are cottages as well as temples. The heart must rest, my dear. Now you must leave me and return to the lake."

"No! Not without you. You are stange and distant. You frighten me, Vegoia!"

"Go now, Arnth. Later I will come to you. I give you my promise."

"What good is a promise in an empty room?"

"The promise of a sorceress is not given lightly. Wait for me, my dear." She pushed him away from her with small, inflexible hands and leaned, soundlessly weeping, against the arbor of vines and dogwood trees. The weight of her body shook the images into a wisp of song, as if the ghosts of birds were singing above the ashen Styx, with dear Charun plying his oar and staring up at them to guess the unheard notes. Evanescent as smoke, she seemed; or an amber flame burning in a cold forest. She did not call to him across that shaken air, but raised her hand in a slow salutation: little girl's hand, sending away her friend of the greenbright summer, waving good-bye.

It was not till he reached the lake that he remembered: in their last embrace, he had felt the unmistakable beating of her heart.

I will cook her a meal, he thought. *I will busy myself with her loved domestic tasks and summon her from the woods. Stir the coals in the oven. Brown the mussels to the color of October. Roast the chestnuts until they crack like snails and exude a fragrance of earth, fire, and air. Vegoia, sorceress, I call to you with the strong magic of familiarity. Conjure you into your old shape, in the old place, beside me.*

He heard the canoe as it brushed against the raft, and his heart leaped like a netted hare.

"Vegoia!"

It was Tanaquil. She had brought him a basket of grapes.

"You see," she said proudly. "They look like swollen amethysts! I practically stole them from the bees. Where is Vegoia?"

"In the forest."

"Alone?"

"Yes."

"You must go and find her!"

"She told me to come here and wait for her."

"Then you must wait. Shall I keep you company?"

"I think she meant for me to wait alone."

Tanaquil nodded with understanding and left him to his vigil.

He waited. Afternoon moved cloudily over the

lake, and dusk settled like a woolen shroud, dark and smothering. Arnza came with the rising of the moon. He dipped and spun and pointed toward the shore.

"Quick, quick," he seemed to say.

Following the sprite as a mariner follows Polaris, he paddled across the lake and moored his canoe among the reeds. The sprite sadly forsook him when he entered the forest. The trees were too thick and tangled for flight.

Here and there, on the floor of jutting roots and fallen pine needles, on the lifted arms of trees, the Lady Moon had strewn her crystal silvers, like shavings from the shop of a Titan lapidary.

"Vegoia!" he called, and thought of her slender feet torn by the roots of the trees, who envied her swiftness and clawed at her flesh with old men's fingers, half to caress, half to wound and destroy. *Sly old men, lecherous oaks and lusting pines: you shall not touch my beloved? Where have you hidden her from me? I will strike a spark to your desecrated limbs, your gray-moss hair which is snarled with birds and bark! I will slash your knotted knees with sword and ax! Where have you hidden the nymph of the waters?*

"Vegoia!"

"V-e-g-o-i-a!" Oak echoes. Pine echoes. Mockery of the trees, rasping back to him the loved, inviolate name. An owl hooted visibly among the branches. A cat-shape slouched across his path (one of the cats from Sutrium?); paused insolently to flaunt its contempt of men; and vanished, a yellow-eyed shadow with shadows.

Then he saw her. She stood in a clearing of gagea. Cast in silver, she seemed; the moon's sister, her feet awash in the silverness of flowers.

She smiled but did not approach him. "In a way I have kept my promise. I could not come to you. But I have brought you to me."

He stumbled toward her as she flickered out of his reach. He might have been trying to catch his reflection in a tidepool.

"No, Arnth. You must not try to touch me. I am—changed. I have come to say good-bye."

He stopped. He stammered like a small boy. "W-why do you want to leave me?"

"Leave you? I would battle all the Griffins of the Styx to stay with you for a year, a week, a day! But when has an earthling been allowed to choose his fate? You know as well as I that demons surround us, invisible in the trees, bodiless in the wind. And Gods beyond demons, and some say, a great winged being called Necessity beyond the gods, the Builder, and the universe. We are waxen images in unseen hands. For awhile, we were overlooked, you and I. Or perhaps a god looked down with condescending pity and allowed us a little hour of love, and then grew bored with our antics and took away his gift. Never ask, my dear. I must go now. Be always beautiful!"

"Vegoia," he cried. "It was I who did this to you. I cursed you with a heart. And now it has broken you!"

"I think I have always had a heart. It lay like a fledgling asleep in my breast. It was you who taught it to fly. Cursed, you say? Blessed! I have never cared for sleep."

He reached to touch her and touched a coolness of wind, and the light of her danced beyond him, will-o-the-wisp, flickering through the trees, and he did not know if he pursued a nymph, or a light only, a coolness, handful of wind.

He climbed the hill of the blackberry bushes. He lost the path; his legs caught fire with the thorns. Then, the crest, and emptiness yawned at his feet; the Great Mundus, yawning a pit to the nether lands; a chasm as old as the war between the gods and the Titans, when lightning had gouged the Great Green Sea and cast up the Mountains of Atlas. Precipitous walls, softened a little with shrubs and vines at the rim, fell into blackness beyond the rays of the moon. Perhaps in the heart of the pit lidless eyes of Griffins gleamed like moons, and Charon's oar cut the Styx with phosphorescent stars. But the blackness which met his eyes was moonless, starless, lightless. Night compounded by night.

He found the path. He lurched and stumbled, grasped at the scaly hands held out by roots, and stood at last on a ledge where earthen or wooden sarcophagi hunched in a row, like spawning turtles along a beach at night. But death, not life, was their burden. Figures were sculptured on the lids, half-reclining as if at a banquet. A woman with skin like the underside of a mushroom. An old man with feet like the wings of a bat. A laughing child with a wooden fish in his hands.

Vegoia's sarcophagus had not been closed. She lay like an unlit candle in its narrow gloom. Tomorrow her friends would carve her image in oak or citron wood and shut her from the watching sky. Never mind. Not even the lordly sun could rekindle her light. Not here. But the dark waters of the Styx would shine with more than the phosphorescence of Charon's oars; with as much of light as the candle had lost.

"You have no gift for Charon," he said. "And I have no coin to place on your tongue. But I think he will not deny you a passage."

The wagon lay on its back like a horseshoe crab, its carapace slashed with knives, and its entrails strewn in the shape of clothes and furnishings. A Veientine army, equipped with siege towers and battering rams, had recaptured Sutrium, and the Fauns and Centaurs, leaving the slaves to the justice of the conquerors, had fled to the woods in fury and vented their wrath on this handiwork of man.

Still, Arnth found, the wreckage was not irreparable. With the help of the Water Sprites, he righted the cart and mended the tattered canopy. With the help of those other sprites, Arnza and his friends, he fitted the bare interior with a pallet of animal skins, while Tanaquil wove a coverlet out of flamingo feathers.

Now, it was time to depart for Rome, the valorous little town which had recently exiled its Etruscan king, Tarquin the Proud, and delcared its independence. The sprites sang and capered as he and Tanaquil took their seats. There were garlands around his neck, Tanaquil's hair had become a garden of roses, and honeysuckle entwined the canopy and seemed to heal the recently mended tears.

"It's like harvest festival," she whispered. "They might be carrying sheaves instead of flowers."

He frowned. "It's much too soon to sing. Have they forgotten her so easily?" To Arnth at least, brightness had gone from the Town of Walking Towers; swiftness from the waters. Scarcely a month had passed, and yet her people sang.

"Remember what she told you about Vel: 'Don't judge him. He is what he has always been.' "

"I know," he said. "I know. I do love them in spite of their lightness. It's just that I want them to be like her."

"No one is."

Ursus was in his harness, submissive, no longer irascible. He hardly seemed to care that he had lost the patch from his eye, or that sprites had insisted on twining honeysuckle around his prodigious neck. *He is getting old*, though Arnth. *When we get to Rome, I will build a room for him, with a bed of straw and a honey pot filled to the brim.*

He had to flick the reins to catch the bear's attention. Ursus was not being stubborn. It was just that he seemed preoccupied. He was missing Vegoia.

"Farewell, Arnth!"

"Farewell, Tanaquil!"

"Mellonia sweeten your path!"

The wheels, liberally greased with olive oil, began to turn; the cart groaned into motion and rolled with quickening speed toward Sutrium, Veii, and liberated Rome. Behind and ahead of them marched the Water Sprites; martial now, vigilant for Fauns and Centaurs among the trees; guarding their human friends out of the Weirwoods. Above them the Corn Sprites wheeled in fiery arcs, and Arnza dipped from the sky to tap Arnth's nose with a last homely gesture of farewell.

"Good-bye, little friend," Arnth cried, and Arnza's smile grew mischievous as if to say: "If I see a Faun, I'll spit in his ear for you!"

Tanaquil sat beside him as quietly as a statue.

Her tunic became her. In the weeks on the lake she had tanned and hardened to the brown suppleness of a nymph. Except for her dusky hair and her grave, thoughtful silence, she might have been one of the sprites.

"Are you sure to want to come to Rome with me?" he asked. "Any Etruscan city would be proud to accept the daughter of Lars Velcha. I would stay, if you liked, until you were settled."

"You wouldn't be happy. Etruscans would always treat you like a traveling player. Or a Gaul. But in Rome, you could feel at home, couldn't you?"

"Yes," he admitted. "The Romans are like me. Farmers and traveling players and not princes and slaves. I will build a house, plant some grain, and keep a few pigs. And fight, of course, if Tarquin makes war on us to get back his throne. And sing. I still have my flute, you know. I found it under the wagon."

"I'll go to Rome," she said. "I understand that there's a shortage of women. Didn't the first Romans have to steal their mates from the Sabines?"

"But that was a long time ago."

"How do you know there isn't still a shortage?"

"That's their problem," said Arnth firmly. "You're with me."

"Am I, Arnth?"

She placed a hand on his arm. It was a comfortable hand. What had Vegoia said? "It is the measure of a man that he can move from woodfire to hearthfire without bitterness, without reproaching the gods, his enemies, or himself." He would never forget that brief, bright burning in a wintry forest, the blue and the amber.

But hearthfires were also good.

ACE SCIENCE FICTION SPECIALS

10150	**Challenge The Hellmaker** Richmond $1.25
20660	**Endless Voyage** Bradley $1.25
21430	**Equality in the Year 2000** Reyndds $1.50
25461	**From the Legend of Biel** Staton $1.50
30420	**Growing Up In the Tier 3000** Gotschalk $1.25
37171	**The Invincible** Lem $1.50
46850	**Lady of the Bees** Swann $1.25
66780	**A Plague of All Cowards** Barton $1.50
71160	**Red Tide** Chapman & Tarzan $1.25
81900	**Tournament of Thorns** Swann $1.50

Available wherever paperbacks are sold or use this coupon.

ace books, (Dept. MM) Box 576, Times Square Station
New York, N.Y. 10036

Please send me titles checked above.

I enclose $.................. Add 35c handling fee per copy.

Name ....

Address ....

City..................... State.............. Zip........

64B